THE
SECRET SEVEN

MYSTERY OF THE SKULL

Have you read all
THE SECRET SEVEN books?

And don't miss:
SECRET SEVEN BRAIN GAMES –
a fun and tricky puzzle book

Enid Blyton

THE
SECRET
SEVEN

MYSTERY OF THE SKULL

WRITTEN BY **PAMELA BUTCHART**

ILLUSTRATED BY **Tony Ross**

h

Hodder
Children's
Books

For Albie, with all my love. I promise to make sure your life is full of fun adventures.

HODDER CHILDREN'S BOOKS

First published in Great Britain in 2018 by Hodder & Stoughton

1 3 5 7 9 10 8 6 4 2

The Secret Seven®, Enid Blyton® and Enid Blyton's signature are
registered trade marks of Hodder & Stoughton Limited
Written by Pamela Butchart. Text © 2018 Hodder & Stoughton Limited
Illustrated by Tony Ross. Illustrations © 2018 Hodder & Stoughton Limited

A CIP catalogue record for this book is available from the British Library.

ISBN 978 1 444 94153 1

Typeset in Caslon Twelve by Avon DataSet Ltd, Bidford-on-Avon, Warwickshire

Printed and bound by CPI Group (UK) Ltd, Croydon, CR0 4YY

The paper and board used in this book are made from wood from responsible sources.

CONTENTS

CHAPTER ONE

A NEW MYSTERY

IT HAD been ages since the last Secret Seven meeting. In fact, it had been so long that there was a huge spiderweb right across the door of the shed at the bottom of the garden.

'We'll need to get rid of that,' said Peter. 'Go on,' he said, looking at Jack.

Jack looked a bit freaked out. 'But it's got big hairy bits stuck to it,' he mumbled.

That's when Janet, Peter's sister, pushed past them and ripped the giant spiderweb in two with her bare hands.

Peter and Jack stared at her.

'Are you coming in?' Janet said. 'Or have you forgotten that this is an emergency meeting? You're not scared of spiders, are you?'

Peter walked in slowly, very carefully stepping round the remains of the sticky web.

'We can't start the meeting until everyone gets here anyway,' he said.

Just then George arrived and his face was bright red and he was panting. 'Sorry! Sorry I'm late!' he puffed, even though he was actually right on time.

Jack began wiping down the boxes and upturned flowerpots and asking about food because Janet and Peter's mum always made them snacks when they were having an official meeting.

'There wasn't time to wait for my mum to finish making the sandwiches,' said Peter. 'This is urgent!'

Jack gasped. There was always time for snacks.

'But I'm starving!' he said. 'I didn't have breakfast because you came up to my house so early and basically pulled me out of bed, Peter!'

And then he ran out of the shed and up to Peter and Janet's house before Peter could argue with him.

Peter looked at his watch and started pacing backwards and forwards, shaking his head. He had sent out a message saying that the meeting started at 9 a.m. sharp and it was now 9.02 a.m.

He was just about to say that he was seriously considering turning the Secret Seven into the Secret Four when Jack appeared back in the doorway with a plate of sandwiches and biscuits and Colin.

That's when Peter shut the shed door right in their faces.

'HEY! There's no need for that!' Jack shouted from the other side of the door.

'What's the password?' asked Peter.

Peter was getting on Jack's nerves.

'ARMPIT!' he shouted.

That made Peter furious because the password definitely wasn't Armpit and he knew Jack was just saying that to annoy him because he'd shut the door in his face (and also because he'd probably forgotten the real password like he always did).

But before Peter could say anything about the Armpit thing, Colin said, 'Scotland! The password is Scotland.'

Peter opened the door and gave Jack a look. Jack grinned back at him and went and took a seat next to Janet and started eating a jam sandwich.

But the Secret Seven still couldn't start the meeting because Pam and Barbara weren't there yet and everyone knew that they would be at least ten minutes late and that Peter would be raging about it because that's what always happened.

'Come and sit down and tell us what's going on,' said Jack, already munching on his second sandwich.

But Peter was too busy staring out of the peephole in the shed wall and muttering to himself about Pam and Barbara.

Jack rolled his eyes. 'Janet, what's going on?'

But before Janet could answer there was scratching at the shed door and George almost jumped out of his skin because Janet had just finished telling

Colin about the whole giant web thing.

Everyone froze and listened to the creepy scratching sound.

'It's probably just Scamper,' said Jack.

Janet shook her head and pointed to the corner of the shed where Scamper was already curled up asleep.

George gulped.

But then they heard giggling and a voice said, '*Wooooooooo!* Let us in or we'll scratch the door down with our witchy nails!'

Peter rolled his eyes. 'What's the password?'

'*Scoooootland,*' another voice said. It was Barbara.

Everyone burst out laughing when Pam and Barbara walked in because they were dressed up as witches and Barbara had even drawn warts all over her face with pen.

But Peter wasn't laughing. He had his arms crossed and looked mega annoyed, and everyone knew that it wasn't just because Pam and Barbara were late. It was because they were wearing fancy dress to an official Secret Seven meeting.

'Are you two off to a fancy-dress party?' asked Janet.

'No,' said Barbara. 'We just felt like being witches today.'

Peter shook his head. 'You'll soon stop thinking everything's so funny when I tell you what I found last night.'

Peter sat down on his chair, got out his official Secret Seven notebook and took a deep breath.

'I've called this meeting of the Secret Seven Society to discuss something seriously weird.'

As soon as Peter said that, Pam and Barbara shut up and stared at him.

That's when Peter explained that he and Janet had arrived home the night before from staying with their gran for the first fortnight of the summer holidays.

'When I went up to my room, I got a strange

feeling the minute I opened the door,' he said. 'I just knew that someone had been in there while I'd been gone.'

Everyone leant forward as Peter took something out of his backpack and placed it on the ground in front of them.

'And then I found this.'

Pam and Barbara gasped, and George actually moved his flowerpot back a bit.

Jack looked at Peter with wide eyes. 'Peter, is this a joke?'

But Peter didn't even need to answer because this was obviously not a joke.

This was real.

And they all knew that it was up to them to do something right away.

Because it was a *skull*!

CHAPTER TWO

THE PETER SKULL

NO ONE had any idea where the skull could have come from or why it had been in Peter's bedroom.

Colin inspected the skull closely.

'It's only half a skull,' he said. 'I think it looks human. But I can't be sure without the other half.'

Janet leant forward and scrunched up her eyes. 'What's that? There's something written on it.'

She took her torch out of her bag and shone it on the skull.

'There's too much dirt. I can't read it properly.'

'Um, maybe it's, you know, *his* name,' said George, pointing at the skull with a shaky finger.

'Maybe it's not dirt,' said Jack. 'Maybe it's blood!'

Pam gasped and grabbed Barbara's hand.

Janet wiped the skull with her sleeve. 'I think it says Peter,' she said.

'This is too weird,' said Jack. 'I need a biscuit.'

Jack shoved a whole ginger biscuit in his mouth and then passed the plate to Pam but she said that she didn't want one because the Peter Skull was making her feel a bit sick.

All of a sudden George drew in a huge breath. 'What if it's a warning?'

'What do you mean?' said Peter.

George swallowed the rest of his biscuit with a loud gulp. 'I think someone might have put the skull there as a threat. They might be trying to warn you off something.'

Just then they heard a noise outside.

'Did anyone else hear that?' Jack whispered.

Everyone nodded.

Peter got up and looked out of the peephole. But he couldn't see anyone.

Then there was another sound. It sounded like it was coming from the roof.

'I don't like this,' said Pam. 'We need to get rid of the skull. It's probably cursed!'

'Sssssssh!' said Janet. 'I hear something.'

'That's it,' said Peter. 'I'm going out. If there is someone there, it's obviously me they're after.'

He opened the shed door and ran outside. But there was no one there.

'PETER!' Pam yelled. 'Come back inside. What if it's a *headless skeleton*?'

Someone burst out laughing.

Peter looked up at the roof. It was Jack's annoying little sister Susie and her even *more* annoying friend Binkie.

'Get down from there, both of you!' he demanded.

'JACK!' yelled Peter. 'You'd better get out here!'

'Yes, *Jack*,' said Susie. 'You'd better get out here and do *everything* your precious leader tells you to do. That's a good boy.'

Jack was furious. 'Get down NOW!' he said. 'Or I'll tell Mum you were climbing on Peter and Janet's mum's property and you'll be grounded for life!'

'Oh, calm your pants,' said Susie, jumping down. 'We're only having a laugh.'

'*Yeah*, Peter! We're only having a *laugh*!' said Binkie.

'Haven't the two of you got anything better to do than sneak about, spying on us?' Peter said.

'Oh! We've got plenty of exciting things to do,' said Susie. 'Like looking for that *headless skeleton* that's supposedly running around your farm!'

Binkie burst out laughing. 'The headless skeleton strikes again!' she squealed.

Peter narrowed his eyes at Susie. 'It was you, wasn't it?'

'Don't know what you're talking about, King Peter,' said Susie, folding her arms.

'Did YOU put that skull in Peter's bedroom?' Jack shouted. 'How did you even get in?'

Susie smirked. 'Mum was watering their plants while they were away. I might have gone along to help.'

'That's it!' said Jack, storming off. 'I'm telling Mum!'

'Wait!' said Susie. 'Don't you want to know where I found old Peter the skull?'

Jack stopped and looked at Peter.

'Ha! I thought that might interest you. It might even be the next big case for the totally *wonderful* Secret Seven!' she said sarcastically. 'THE MYSTERY OF THE SKULL!' she shrieked at the top of her lungs.

Peter rolled his eyes. Why did Jack have to have such an annoying little sister?

'Where did you find it?' asked Peter.

'How much is it worth to you?' said Susie.

Jack marched back over. 'I'll tell you exactly how much it's worth. Either you tell us where you found it *now* or I'll tell Mum you sneaked into Peter's room and left a skull there. I'll also tell her what really happened to the Hoover. How about that?'

'*Fine!*' said Susie. 'We found it down near the hotel.'

'What were you doing down there?' asked Jack.

'Just taking a look around,' said Susie. 'We wanted to see what the new owners looked like. They're American.'

'I said they might be famous film stars!' said Binkie.

'And are they?' asked Peter.

Susie shrugged. 'We didn't see anyone except old Peter the skull.'

'You'd better not be lying to us about where you found it, Susie,' said Peter.

'We're not!' said Binkie. 'Someone's been digging there. Go and see for yourself!'

CHAPTER THREE

SOMEONE SUSPICIOUS

AS SOON as the Secret Seven got close to the hotel grounds, Peter hissed, 'Get down!' and everyone dropped to the ground, just like he had trained them to do.

'What is it? What's going on?' whispered Jack.

Peter lay flat in the long grass and pointed ahead.

There was a figure in the distance.

'Someone's digging,' he whispered back. 'We need to get closer to get a better look. Follow me.'

The Secret Seven followed Peter carefully, staying as low to the ground as they could. But then Scamper started barking and ran through a gap in the wire fencing straight towards the digging man.

'Scamper! Come back!' Peter cried. But Scamper kept on running so Janet ran after him.

'Is this your dog trespassing on my land?'

That's when Janet noticed that the digging man was actually a woman with a weird accent, and also that she was absolutely covered in mud.

All of a sudden the muddy woman rushed towards Scamper but Janet got there first. 'What does he have there? What's in his mouth?' the woman demanded.

'It's just a stick,' said Janet.

Peter arrived and apologised about Scamper and asked if she was the new owner of the hotel. And that's when the woman completely changed.

'Oh, yes! Yes! I *am* the new owner,' she said with a massive grin. 'My husband and I have come all the way from the USA to be here. We just love the English countryside!'

'My uncle's got a new job at your restaurant. He says there's loads of people booked to come to your big opening tomorrow. No wonder! Everyone in the village was very excited when they saw all the adverts for it.'

The muddy woman looked flustered. 'Yes. Well. Um. We may have to close the restaurant for a few days after the opening. There's still a bit of decorating to do.'

But then the muddy woman noticed everyone staring at the giant hole next to her. 'I've just been doing a little weeding,' she said.

The Secret Seven watched as she moved herself in front of the hole so that they couldn't see it properly.

'Better get back to it!' she said.

The woman stood there, giving them a weird, fake-looking smile.

It was obvious she wanted them gone, so Peter said goodbye and they left.

But Janet didn't trust the muddy woman one bit. She didn't like the way she'd rushed towards Scamper like that and the look she'd had on her face.

Janet turned round to take one last look at the woman as they walked away.

The muddy woman wasn't smiling any more. And she wasn't weeding either.

She was staring at them as they walked off.

And she did not look happy.

CHAPTER FOUR

A MIDNIGHT MISSION

AS SOON as they got back to the shed, Janet lifted up her jumper and another skull fell out and on to the floor.

Everyone gasped.

'That's what Scamper really had in his mouth,' she said. 'I stuck it up my jumper before that woman could see.'

'Well done, Janet!' said Peter. 'Our second piece of evidence. Brilliant!'

But then Scamper grabbed the evidence and it took Peter and Janet ages to get it out of his mouth. In the end they had to give him a biscuit just so he'd let go.

Colin wiped dog drool off the skull and held it

up against the first skull they'd found.

'Well,' he said, pushing up his glasses. 'It's obviously not part of the same skull. They don't fit together at all. This must be part of another skull.'

Pam's eyes went wide. 'You don't think she's burying human skulls, do you?'

Barbara gasped.

'I don't think so,' said Colin. 'These skulls look like they've been buried for a while. They're all cracked. I think it's more likely she dug these up.'

'Why would she be digging up old skulls?' asked Pam. 'That's totally creepy! And why would there be human skulls buried there anyway?'

George gasped. 'My granddad once told me that our village is built on top of an Ancient Roman village. Maybe the hotel was built on top of a graveyard!'

Pam gasped. '*What?* So for all we know there could be ancient graves underneath our whole village? There might even be some buried under the shed!'

George shrugged. 'There might be.'

As soon as George said that, Pam and Barbara both lifted their feet up so they weren't touching the ground.

Peter rolled his eyes.

'I wonder if she dug the skulls up by accident while she was digging that big hole,' said Janet.

That's when Janet told everyone about how the woman had run towards Scamper and how she had seemed panicked about what Scamper might have found.

'It was like she didn't want Scamper to find something – like she had something to hide,' said Janet. 'I mean, it was obvious she didn't want us to see inside the hole. And there was no way she was just weeding. That hole was huge!'

Barbara nodded her head loads. 'Did you notice how she completely changed and started being all nice to us when Peter asked if she was the new hotel owner?' she said. 'That was weird.'

Everyone agreed that the American woman had been acting strangely and that she'd been lying about the weeding.

So Peter took out his notebook and wrote:

Clue 1: Skull found in my bedroom
Clue 2: Part of a second skull found in hotel grounds
Clue 3: New hotel owner behaving suspiciously and digging large hole

Then Jack took a deep breath and said, 'We need to go back there and see what's in that hole . . . *tonight*.'

That night the Secret Seven met at the shed at midnight.

'Wait for us!' hissed Pam and Barbara just as the other five were about to set off on their bikes.

'We didn't think you were coming,' said Colin.

'Almost got caught,' puffed Barbara. 'We had to

jump back into bed and pretend to be sleeping until my mum started snoring. Pam's staying over at mine.'

Pam and Barbara were both wearing bright pink pyjamas and Barbara still had her slippers on.

'You were supposed to wear black,' said Peter. 'You'll be spotted a mile away!'

Jack started laughing at the state of Pam and Barbara. 'Only the two of you would wear pyjamas on a midnight mission!'

'It's fine. No one will see them,' Janet said. 'Everyone's asleep. Let's go.'

The Secret Seven set off on their bikes through the dark field towards the hotel.

But the closer they got the mistier it became and they had to slow down because it was becoming difficult to see.

George stopped his bike. 'I don't like this. There might be ghosts around that aren't very happy about their skulls being dug up! I'm going back.'

But no one else wanted to go back (and George was too scared to go back on his own).

'It's fine,' Peter said. 'I think we're pretty much here.'

He got off his bike and shone his torch around. 'Look! There's the broken fence Scamper ran through.'

Peter turned his torch towards the others and gave them a serious look.

'Right, torches stay off as soon as we enter the hotel grounds. OK? And we leave the bikes here.'

'Um . . . maybe some of us should stay here, with the bikes,' said George nervously. 'So they don't get stolen or anything.'

Peter knew that the bikes would be fine but seeing George's frightened face he said, 'Good idea, George. If you see anyone coming, give us the Get Out signal. OK? Pam and Barbara, you can stay too since you're not exactly wearing camouflage.'

But Pam and Barbara didn't want to stay. So,

after a bit of an argument, Colin said that he would stay with George and the rest of them set off on foot.

'Wait for me! I can't see a thing!' hissed Pam. 'Peter! Put the torch on!'

'Shhhh!' Peter hissed. 'You're going to get us caught!'

'What if one of us falls into the hole, Peter? What then? Did you ever think of that?' said Barbara.

Peter stopped. He hadn't thought of that actually, and he was just about to turn the torch on when Barbara gasped.

Everyone froze.

'What? What is it?' Peter hissed.

'There's mud in my slippers! Oh, *yuck*, I can feel it between my toes!'

Peter was starting to get really annoyed. 'What did you think was going to happen? You're wearing *pug slippers* in the middle of a muddy field at midnight, Barbara!'

Jack started laughing a bit too loudly.

'Everyone quiet,' Janet whispered. 'Look!'

They all stopped and looked.

'Is that a tent?' said Pam.

The mist had cleared and now they could see a large tent covering the exact spot where the American woman had been digging earlier. It looked like one of those big white marquee things that people have parties in.

'She's trying to hide the hole,' Janet whispered. 'Very clever.'

Janet looked up at the hotel. All the lights were off.

'Let's go inside that tent and have a look at what she's been up to.'

Peter nodded and they all moved quickly towards it.

'Follow me,' whispered Jack. 'I think the entrance is round this way.'

But then all of a sudden a light went on inside

the tent and Jack got such a fright he slipped and fell with a splat.

Everyone froze (even Jack, who was lying face down in the mud).

'Get down!' whispered Peter.

They crouched down in the mud and watched as the light moved round the side of the tent.

Someone was in there.

Someone had heard them!

And then Barbara took off her slippers and hissed, 'Run!'

CHAPTER FIVE

JANET COMES UP WITH A PLAN

THE NEXT day, everyone was late for the meeting. Even Peter!

'I barely slept a wink last night,' said Barbara as she burst into the shed and flopped down on the rug next to Scamper. 'Every time I closed my eyes I kept imagining millions of worms wriggling between my toes!'

Jack burst out laughing, spraying sponge cake everywhere.

'It's not funny!' Barbara snapped. 'I was covered in mud when I got home. I had to have a bath in the dark so I didn't wake anyone up. I'd be grounded for life if my mum found out I'd sneaked out!'

'Hey!' said Jack. 'You weren't the only one covered

in mud, you know. I actually *swallowed* some of it when I fell. That's way worse!'

Barbara shrugged.

'I suppose that's why you're eating all the cake then? To get rid of the mud taste?' said Janet.

Jack grinned. 'Absolutely!'

Peter cleared his throat and everyone turned and looked at him.

'We've all had a rough night,' he said. 'Me and Janet had to sleep in the shed and sneak back into the house this morning once my dad went out to work on the farm because *someone* forgot to flip the latch on the back door when we sneaked out last night.'

Janet's face went bright red. She'd made one tiny mistake but Peter was never going to let her forget it.

Peter took out the official Secret Seven notebook. 'OK, so who do we think was inside the tent last night?'

'I think it was the American woman,' said Barbara.
Pam and Jack nodded.

'We can't be sure of that,' said Janet.

'But that's where we saw her digging the hole earlier,' said Barbara.

Janet nodded. 'Yes, but all we saw last night was a torch. It could have been anyone in there.'

'Well, whoever it was, it's all a bit suspicious,' said Peter. 'Why would someone be in a tent in the middle of the night?'

'Maybe someone was camping,' said Colin. 'The new owners might have let someone use their ground to camp.'

'I still think it was the American woman,' said Barbara. 'I think she might be digging up ancient skeletons on purpose!'

Peter shook his head. 'That doesn't make any sense, Barbara. Why would she want ancient skeletons?'

Barbara sat up straight. 'Maybe she's a witch! Witches use bones,' she said.

Pam gasped and Peter rolled his eyes. 'You two are obsessed with witches! Forget it. She's not a witch.'

Colin stood up and walked around. 'Wait a minute. Barbara might be on to something actually.'

Peter couldn't believe what he was hearing. Witches? Witches weren't even real!

'I read a history book in the library that said witches used animal bones instead of spoons or sticks to stir their potions,' said Colin.

Barbara stood up. 'That's it! She's digging up skeletons for her spells!'

Peter buried his head in his hands. He'd had enough of this nonsense. He was exhausted. He'd hardly slept all night, thinking about where the skulls might have come from.

'Does anyone have any other ideas?' he said. 'Any *non-witch* ideas, I mean?'

Jack pulled his flowerpot closer to the middle of the group. 'I'm not sure, but I think we should go back to the hotel and get a look inside the tent and the hotel, if we can. But I'm not sure how we're going to get away with that.'

Janet smiled. 'I do. I've made a plan,' she said. And she looked right at Peter as she said it. She wanted him to know that yes, she might have made one tiny mistake with the door latch but that didn't mean she couldn't come up with a brilliant plan.

'Oh!' said Peter. 'Well, let's hear it then.'

'Well, as you know, it's my birthday tomorrow,' said Janet.

Peter tried not to show that he was panicking inside. He'd completely forgotten about his sister's birthday. *Again!* She was going to kill him.

'So I spoke to Mum this morning and guess where we're all going for my birthday dinner tomorrow?'

Peter looked at Janet blankly. He had no idea where they were going. But he hoped it was somewhere with a shop so he could buy her a last-minute gift with the money his gran had given him.

32

Janet smiled. 'Mum and Dad are taking all seven of us to the new hotel restaurant for my birthday dinner! That should get us close enough to do a bit of snooping without anyone noticing, shouldn't it?'

Peter smiled at Janet.

She knew what he was thinking, even if he wouldn't say it out loud.

She. Was. A. Genius.

CHAPTER SIX

THE FISH PIE DISASTER

THE HOTEL restaurant looked really nice inside and it didn't seem like there was any decorating left to do.

Everyone had dressed up and brought gifts and Janet and Peter's mum said that they could order whatever they wanted from the menu. Janet almost forgot why they were really there.

But then the weird American woman appeared. She looked different when she wasn't covered in mud. Her hair was wild and curly and she was wearing a ton of make-up.

'HI, GUYS! WELCOME!' she boomed. 'I hear it's someone's birthday today, is that right?'

But then she spotted Janet.

'Oh. It's you.'

Her smile dropped. Just for a second. But they all noticed.

'We meet again!' she said, slapping a big smile across her face.

The Secret Seven watched as the woman made her way round the table, laying down menus and avoiding eye contact with them.

Then, just as she was about to head back into the kitchen, Mum said, 'Thanks very much for having us at short notice for Janet's birthday. How are you finding the village so far?'

The American woman whizzed round. She'd plastered another super-fake smile across her face.

'No problem! We absolutely adore the English countryside. It's *totally awesome*! Such a change from the USA. It's all skyscrapers and traffic jams where we're from.'

'Glad to hear it,' said Mum. 'Just let us know if you ever need anything. We live on the farm there, just over the field,' she said, pointing out of the window towards the farmhouse.

The American woman smiled and cast a quick glance at Janet. 'Is that so?' she said.

Peter looked at Janet. Janet knew exactly what he was thinking because she was thinking the same thing. Their mum had just told this woman where they lived. And, if it turned out they were right and that she was a criminal, then that was bad news.

Suddenly Janet had an idea.

'So, when is the big occasion?' she asked the woman sweetly. 'Is it a wedding?'

The woman looked at her blankly.

'The big tent out back?' said Janet. 'We thought it might be for a wedding or something.'

The woman's eyes went wide. 'Oh. Um. YES! We're hosting a wedding this weekend.'

'Wow,' said Janet. 'You must be busy!'

The woman looked mega annoyed that Janet was still asking questions about the tent.

'Yes, yes,' she said. 'Our party planner is out there now, setting up. Lots to do!'

The woman thanked Mum and rushed back into the kitchen.

George let out a big sigh. He'd been holding his breath.

Jack turned the menu round in his hands. Then he picked up Colin's menu and did the same. 'Where's the rest of it?' he asked.

Everyone looked at their menus. They weren't even really menus. They were small bits of lined paper with only one thing written on them: FISH PIE

Mum got up and went to ask about the menu.

Colin leant over the table. 'This is weird. Why is there only one thing on the menu?'

Just then Mum came back and said that the only meal the kitchen would be cooking today was homemade fish pie and pasta for anyone who was vegetarian.

Janet and Peter's dad rolled his eyes. He looked just like Peter when he did it. 'It's going to be one of those places, is it? Well, it'd better be a decent fish pie. That's all I've got to say about it!'

Jack's jaw dropped. 'Wait. Does that mean no dessert?'

Janet's mum laughed. 'Don't worry. I asked about that. Mrs Lockheart says there's ice cream for afters.'

Jack relaxed back into his chair. He didn't think he'd be able to focus on the mission properly if Janet's mum hadn't said that. He needed sugar!

George took a pen out of his pocket and wrote something down on his napkin and then stuffed it up his sleeve.

'It's almost eight fifteen,' Peter whispered to Janet.

Janet nodded and gave Pam the Look.

Pam gave Janet the Look back.

It was almost time to start Part One of the plan.

Janet had asked her mum to book the dinner for

8 p.m. because Pam had said that people go to restaurants later than they have dinner at home and they all knew that the restaurant would have to be full for them to get away with their plan.

Janet watched closely as more and more people came in to try the new hotel restaurant. Almost every table was taken by 8.10 p.m.

'Pssst! Look over there,' Colin said.

The American woman was standing speaking to a huge bald man. The man gave her a quick kiss on the head. They both looked a bit worried about something.

'That must be her husband,' said Peter.

All of a sudden smoke started coming out of the kitchen. The woman went running back inside while her husband headed out into the hallway.

Janet could hear the other guests talking about the menu and the fish pie. No one seemed very happy about it.

After a few minutes the American woman poked

her head out from the kitchen. Her face was bright red.

'BE WITH Y'ALL IN JUST A SEC!' she yelled before disappearing back inside.

Colin looked around. 'Where are all the waiters and people who work here? Where's your uncle, Pam?'

Pam smiled. 'He'll be in the kitchen. He's the head cook!'

Janet's dad gave Pam a quick smile and Pam knew it was because of what he'd said a minute ago about the fish pie and how it'd better be good.

'Don't worry!' Pam shouted down the table so Janet's dad could hear her. 'My uncle's a brilliant cook. He made all the food for his own wedding and it was yummy!'

Just then the American woman came rushing out of the kitchen with two plates of fish pie and gave them to Mum and Dad. Then she ran off and came back a few seconds later with another two and then another two until everyone had been served.

'ENJOY!' she practically screamed, before dashing round the rest of the tables, taking orders and bringing out more fish pie.

Everyone stared at their fish pie. It did not look good.

Pam smiled nervously. 'It'll taste better than it looks. Promise.'

Everyone watched as Pam took the first bite and began to chew.

She froze.

Jack passed her a glass of water and she took it and drank it all really fast.

The fish pie was *horrendous*. The potato topping was completely burnt and the inside was cold and sticky.

Colin's pasta wasn't much better. It actually made a crunching sound when he chewed!

Even though Janet's birthday meal had been a

cover to get everyone to the hotel so they could sneak around and look for clues, Peter couldn't help feeling bad about the horrible food.

Just then the American woman appeared. 'ALL GOOD? YES?' she yelled.

But before anyone could answer Pam turned in her chair. 'Is my uncle working tonight? His name's Jim. He's the head chef.'

The woman's smile slid right off her sweaty face.

'No. Jim doesn't work here,' she said and then she rushed back to the kitchen.

Pam looked stunned. 'That doesn't make any sense!'

Jack leant forward. 'Do we really have to eat this, Peter?'

Peter nodded sadly.

'It might blow our cover if we don't. We can't risk drawing attention to ourselves.'

Jack watched as Peter took another bite. He had tears in his eyes. That's how bad it was.

Janet checked her watch. It was 8.15 p.m.

'I'm just nipping to the loo,' Janet said to no one in particular.

'Oh. I'll come with you,' said Pam, winking.

'Me too!' said Barbara.

Peter gave Janet a look. Barbara pretending to need the loo at 8.15 p.m. wasn't part of the plan. Janet shrugged. There was nothing they could do now.

Peter grabbed Janet's hand as she was leaving. 'Good luck,' he whispered.

As soon as they were in the corridor, Barbara made a face. 'Sorry! I just really need to wee!'

'It's fine,' said Janet. 'You can go with Pam. I'm going back the way we came in,' she said. 'You two go the other way, OK?'

Pam and Barbara nodded.

'Meet you back at the table in five minutes max,' Janet whispered. 'And remember, if you get caught—'

'We were looking for the toilet,' Pam said quickly.

Janet nodded and watched Pam and Barbara head down the corridor and out of sight. Now it was her turn. She made sure no one was around and then walked down the main steps of the hotel, out into the garden and round the back.

The tent looked even bigger in the daylight than it had the night before.

Janet checked no one was looking and then raced across the lawn and hid behind the tent.

She waited a minute, catching her breath and looking out to the field. She could see the spot where they'd left their bikes the night before.

Then she slowly made her way round the tent, looking for the entrance. But when she turned the last corner she saw the bald man from the restaurant standing at the entrance, holding a shovel.

He definitely didn't look like a party planner!

Janet ducked back round the side of the tent and stood completely still. There was no noise. She was OK. He hadn't seen her.

But then she heard squelchy footsteps coming towards her.

So she ran.

CHAPTER SEVEN

ROOM 101

BY THE time Janet returned to the table almost six minutes had passed and Pam and Barbara weren't back yet.

Peter looked at the mud splashes on Janet's shoes and tights and gave her a worried look.

Just then Pam and Barbara walked into the dining room, smiling and laughing, and sat down at the table as though nothing had happened and they hadn't just been on a spying mission.

Pam looked over at Janet and winked.

Janet smiled. They must have found something.

'HOW MANY ICE CREAMS?' the American woman yelled, bursting out of the kitchen.

All the guests stared at her. She looked like she'd

been in a fight with a fish pie.

She even had some in her hair!

Most of the guests were shaking their heads and some of them were leaving before their food had been served.

Mum looked at Janet. She wasn't keen on pudding after the fish pie disaster but didn't want to cause a scene on Janet's birthday.

Janet nodded and smiled. She didn't really want ice cream from the fish-pie-disaster kitchen. It would probably come out with bits of old fish pie in it. But she knew that they needed more time to complete Part Two of the plan.

'WE'LL HAVE NINE, PLEASE!' Mum shouted back.

Dad groaned.

Jack leant across the table and spoke under his breath. 'Time to go, Peter. She's so stressed out in the kitchen she'll never notice us.'

Peter nodded and got up and walked out of the

room. A few minutes later Jack followed him.

As soon as Jack appeared in the hall, Peter grabbed him by the arm and pulled him into the space underneath the big staircase.

'Hey! Take it easy, Peter!' Jack cried.

Peter covered Jack's mouth with his hand and pointed above them.

Someone was coming down the stairs.

Peter and Jack crouched in silence until the footsteps disappeared.

'Right,' said Peter. 'Time to get up there and start searching for clues about what the hole might be for.'

'How are we supposed to know which rooms to search?' asked Jack.

Peter shook his head. 'We don't. We just need to try as many as we can before our five minutes are up. We might get lucky.'

Jack let out a laugh. 'If you think finding a room full of human skulls is lucky!'

Peter gave him a look. Jack was going to get them all caught one of these days with his loud laughs.

On Peter's signal the boys crept out from under the stairs and up the staircase towards the hotel rooms on the first floor.

The first door they came to said STORAGE.

'Give it a go!' whispered Peter.

Jack tried the handle but it was locked.

The next door said 101. Peter reached out his hand to see if the handle would move.

'GET AWAY FROM THAT DOOR!' a voice boomed.

Jack grabbed Peter's arm. They'd been caught!

The boys spun round to see the bald man from earlier at the top of the staircase. His face was bright red and sweat was pouring off his head and on to his shoulders. He looked seriously mad.

'What do you think you're doing up here?' he yelled.

'Just looking for the toilet,' said Peter calmly.

It always surprised Jack how relaxed Peter could make his voice sound, even when they'd just been caught trespassing by a huge sweaty guy!

The man glared at them. 'Toilet's down there. By the dining room.'

'Ah,' Peter said. 'Sorry about that.'

'Away you go. NOW!' shouted the man.

He watched as Peter and Jack made their way back down the staircase.

'And don't you be coming up here again! You hear me? Up here's for *guests only*.'

Peter and Jack looked back up the staircase at the man and nodded that they understood.

But they both knew that they absolutely would go up there again.

Because there was obviously something up there that he didn't want them to see.

And they were going to find it!

CHAPTER EIGHT

THE FROZEN FOOD DISCOVERY

THE SECRET SEVEN met at the shed at 11 a.m. the next morning.

Peter and Jack told everyone about what had happened to them in the hotel the evening before.

'There's definitely something that man didn't want us to see,' Peter said.

'You should have seen how angry he was,' Jack added. 'He was shouting at us and he had his fists clenched and everything. He's definitely hiding something.'

George took out the napkin he'd been taking notes on at the restaurant.

'He's called Mr Lockheart,' he said, looking at Peter. 'And the woman is Mrs Lockheart.

I heard your mum say their names.'

Peter nodded at George. You could always trust George to take notes.

Now it was Janet's turn to report back on her spying mission.

So she told them about what had happened at the tent and how Mr Lockheart had been standing in the entrance with a shovel so she couldn't get inside.

Pam looked worried. 'Do you think he saw you as well?'

'I can't be sure,' said Janet. 'But I ran my fastest so probably not.'

Peter looked at Pam and Barbara. 'What about you two? Find anything?'

Pam and Barbara looked at each other and grinned.

'Oooooh, yes,' said Barbara. 'Wait until you see *this*.'

Pam pulled something out of her pocket and handed it to Peter.

It was a scrunched-up piece of paper.

'It's a receipt!' Pam said proudly.

Peter read it:

```
:··········································:
:       FROZENLAND               :
:          STORES                :
:··········································:

----------------------------------------

LARGE FISH PIE x 15                £29.85
VANILLA ICE CREAM
(EXTRA LARGE VALUE TUB) x 6         £6.00
----------------------------------------

TOTAL =                            £35.85
PAID BY CASH
```

Peter looked confused.

'This isn't evidence that the Lockhearts are up to something illegal, Pam.'

THE FROZEN FOOD DISCOVERY

Pam stood up and put her hands on her hips.

'Oh, yes it is, Peter! This proves they can't cook.'

Jack rubbed his stomach. 'I think we knew that already.' He still felt a bit queasy after the fish pie.

'As bad as that pie was, Pam, I don't think it was an actual crime,' said Peter.

Barbara stood up and pointed at Peter.

'You don't understand what we're saying. We're *saying* that the burnt food showed us that they're bad cooks. But the receipt shows us that they *can't* cook!'

Pam nodded her head loads. 'I mean, they brought frozen pies. All they had to do was heat them up and they burnt them. They obviously have no idea how to run a restaurant. That place was a disaster last night! Why would you buy a hotel and open a brand-new restaurant if you can't cook? There's something else too,' said Pam. 'I spoke to my mum about what Mrs Lockheart said about my uncle not working there and she phoned him right away and he told her that he'd been sacked before he even started!'

Pam kept her eyes really wide for ages, looking straight at Peter. So did Barbara. They looked like a pair of weird owls.

'That *is* a bit suspicious,' said Peter. 'Why would they sack your uncle before he'd even started?'

'And we didn't see any other staff there last night except Mr and Mrs Lockheart,' added Colin.

Peter looked at Pam. 'Do you think you and Barbara could go and interview your uncle? Try to find out why he was sacked?'

'Absolutely!' said Pam.

'Good,' said Peter. 'Now we need to make a plan for tonight.'

George gulped. 'What's happening tonight?'

Peter stood up and gave everyone a serious look. 'Tonight we get inside that tent!'

CHAPTER NINE

TRAPPED

AS SOON as the Secret Seven arrived at the hotel, they followed Peter's plan exactly.

Pam and Jack stood guard at each side of the tent while George stayed on the hill near the bikes, ready to give the Get Out signal if he saw any movement within the hotel.

Peter, Janet, Barbara and Colin listened outside the tent for one full minute, just like Peter had said to do, to make sure there was no one inside.

As soon as Peter gave the Go Ahead nod, Janet led the way to the entrance where she'd seen Mr Lockheart.

Janet took a deep breath and reached down to pull up the zip.

It was stuck.

'It won't budge,' she whispered. 'It must be caught on something. I can't see what.'

Peter knew they were going to have to use a torch even though that meant risking getting caught.

'OK, I'm going to flash my torch on and off really quickly,' he said. 'Be ready.'

Colin and Janet crouched down and Peter flashed the torch on and then off again.

'It's a padlock!' said Colin. 'We can't get in.'

'Who puts a padlock on a tent?' hissed Barbara.

'Someone who doesn't want anyone peeking inside, that's who!' said Janet.

'Maybe she *was* telling the truth,' said Barbara. 'Maybe it's all set up for a wedding in there, with fancy silverware and decorations.'

'Well,' said Janet, rummaging around in her backpack, 'there's only one way to find out.'

She got down on her knees and started digging a hole with a small shovel.

TRAPPED

'What are you doing?' asked Barbara.

'We're going under,' said Janet. 'We just need to dig out enough earth so we can slip underneath. Hurry up and help me. Get those metal pegs out so we can lift the tent up a bit.'

Janet dug while the others pulled at the pegs and tried to lift the tent up enough for one of them to commando-crawl under.

'That's enough,' said Janet. 'Right. I'm going in. Peter, pass me my torch – just in case I need it.'

Peter was about to give Janet his speech about keeping all torches off when he saw that she had her don't-even-*think*-about-it-Peter look on her face, so he just handed the torch to her and didn't say anything.

Peter, Colin and Barbara pulled up the side of the tent as far as they could and watched as Janet disappeared underneath.

'Are you OK?' hissed Barbara after a few moments.

But there was no reply.

That's when Barbara started to panic.

'JANET!' she yelled a bit too loudly.

Just then a light went on in the hotel.

'Quick! Hide!' said Colin. And before anyone could stop him he dropped to the ground and slid under the tent too.

Peter knew that there was a serious chance they were going to get caught inside the tent if someone came out to see what was going on. But he also knew he couldn't leave Janet and Colin inside.

'Go!' said Peter, holding up the tent as far as he could.

Barbara slid under and Peter followed.

It was much darker inside the tent than it was outside.

Barbara grabbed Peter's arm and held on tight.

'Janet, where are you?' Peter whispered into the darkness.

'Over here!'

Peter tried to figure out exactly where Janet's

voice was coming from. She sounded far away. The tent was bigger than he realised.

'Wait!' whispered Colin. 'Don't move!'

Peter and Barbara froze.

'Stay *veeeery* still,' said Colin. 'Janet? Are you OK?'

'I'm OK. I've hurt my ankle but I'm OK.'

As soon as Peter heard that Janet was hurt, he switched on his torch.

Colin was standing a few metres away from them.

But Janet was nowhere to be seen.

And there were holes everywhere.

'I'm over here!' Janet called.

Peter slowly made his way across the tent, dodging the holes until he found Janet lying inside one of the biggest holes at the far end of the tent.

Peter jumped into it and helped Janet out.

'Are you OK?'

'I'm fine,' said Janet. 'Just twisted my ankle a bit when I fell. I should have used my torch.'

Janet looked around and gasped. She couldn't believe how many holes there were!

'Oh, *wow*,' she said. 'Looks like I dodged quite a few before I fell in one.'

Peter nodded. Janet was usually the sensible one. When she charged ahead and put herself in danger like this, it felt all wrong.

'OK, so there's definitely not a wedding happening in here, is there?' said Barbara, shining her torch into the muddy holes. 'What a mess!'

'This is a serious operation,' said Colin. 'She's digging up the whole place.'

'Let's see if we can find anything,' said Janet.

Peter shone his torch into one of the holes. It was empty.

Janet began limping around, doing the same, until Barbara whispered, '*Sssssh!* Did you hear that?'

Everyone switched off their torches and stood still in the dark, listening.

It was an owl hooting.

TRAPPED

But they all knew that it wasn't a real owl.

It was George, up on the hill, doing the Get Out signal to warn them.

Someone was coming.

CHAPTER TEN

RUN, SECRET SEVEN! RUN!

PETER KNEW they couldn't put the torches back on, which meant that they wouldn't be able to make it back to where they had crawled into the tent without someone falling into a hole and hurting themselves.

They were trapped.

'Hide!' whispered Colin as he scampered into one of the holes. 'Get in a hole!'

Peter helped Janet get into one of the holes and then he jumped in and lay down beside her.

'I'm not getting in one of those holes!' hissed Barbara. 'They look like *graves*! What if there are more skulls down there?'

'Who's there?' said a voice none of them recognised.

Barbara shut up. She could feel her heart pounding in her chest.

Someone was outside.

Barbara was just about to scream when another voice she didn't recognise said, 'There's no one out here, Trish. You're paranoid. Come back inside.'

Barbara held her breath.

'I think there's someone inside the tent, Stan. You'd better go and check.'

Barbara didn't wait to hear more. She dropped to the ground and rolled into the nearest hole.

'But it's pitch-black out here!' said the second voice. 'Leave it alone. There's no one in the tent.'

'*Fine*. I'll go and get a torch and look myself. Just like I have to do everything around here!'

Janet lay listening to the voices. They definitely didn't belong to the Lockhearts. Their accent sounded a bit like her gran's. They were Scottish. She was sure of it.

The four listened as the voices continued to argue

and then a door slammed shut and the voices stopped.

'They've gone to get a torch,' whispered Peter. 'Let's go!'

He shone his torch around the tent and everyone scrambled out of their holes and under the gap in the tent.

'We'd better find Pam and Jack and get out of here quick!' said Colin.

'There!' said Janet, pointing at the hill.

Peter looked up. George was flashing his torch on and off and in the torchlight he could make out three figures standing on the hill. He smiled. Pam and Jack must have heard the Get Out signal and run back to George before whoever it was could see them.

Just then the back door of the hotel opened with a creak.

'Run!' hissed Colin.

* * *

The Secret Seven burst into the shed.

'Keep the torches off!' cried Pam. 'They might still be following us!'

Everyone switched off their torches and sat panting, trying to catch their breath.

Janet took a towel and put it over her torch and switched it on so they had just enough light to see each other.

'What do you mean following us?' she asked Pam.

Pam gave Jack a look. 'They saw you. They were running after you!'

Peter looked stunned. 'I thought we'd got away without being seen. I didn't even look back!'

'It's a good thing you didn't,' said Jack. 'At one point they were only a few metres behind Janet.'

Janet shivered. She'd had no idea she had been so close to getting caught.

'Don't worry,' said Peter. 'It's dark and we all had our hoods up. They won't have seen our faces.'

'But what if they do know it was us, Peter?' asked

Pam. 'If they followed us all the way back here, they'll know it's us. Your mum told Mrs Lockheart where you live!'

'This is too much,' said Barbara. 'I need to lie down.'

'Don't worry, Pam,' said Peter. 'It wasn't the Lockhearts chasing us anyway.' Peter looked at Pam and Jack. 'I know it was dark but did either of you get a good look at them? Any idea who they might have been?'

Pam gave Peter a weird look. 'It *was* the Lockhearts,' she said.

Jack nodded. 'I heard George's signal and saw Pam running for the hill. Then I saw Mr and Mrs Lockheart coming out of the hotel. So I ran too.'

Peter looked at Janet. She seemed just as confused as he felt. Had there been four people outside the tent? The two people they had heard arguing definitely weren't the Lockhearts!

Barbara sat up. 'That wasn't the Lockhearts

arguing outside the tent,' she said. 'That was someone else.'

Jack shook his head. 'It *was* the Lockhearts,' he said. 'I *saw* them.'

'But we heard them, didn't we?' said Barbara, looking at the others for backup. 'They didn't sound anything like the Lockhearts. They weren't even American!'

Janet and Peter nodded in agreement.

'They were Scottish,' said Janet.

'But that doesn't make any sense,' said Jack. 'There were definitely only two people out there. The Lockhearts.'

Everyone sat in silence, staring at each other for a bit.

Peter rubbed his face. He couldn't make sense of this.

'Maybe there were four people outside the tent but you just couldn't see the other two,' he said. 'It was dark after all.'

Jack shook his head. 'No, Peter. It was definitely the Lockhearts arguing outside the tent. The security light above the back door was shining right on them when they walked out. It was them.'

'But we would have heard them if they were arguing,' said Barbara. 'Just like we heard the Scottish couple arguing.'

That's when Colin stood up and whispered, '*Shhhhhh!* I think there's someone out there.

'Look at Scamper,' he said.

Scamper was staring at the shed door with his ears perked up.

Janet switched off her torch.

The Secret Seven sat in darkness, listening, as footsteps got closer and closer to the shed.

There was someone out there.

Scamper started to growl.

'They found us,' whimpered Pam.

Peter stood up slowly. There was a bolt on the inside of the shed door that he'd put on to stop

Susie from barging in during their meetings. He knew there probably wasn't enough time to get across to the other side of the shed and lock them inside before whoever was outside reached the shed door but he had to try.

But before Peter could move another muscle the shed door burst open and Pam started screaming.

CHAPTER ELEVEN

GEORGE'S ADVENTURE

EVERYONE GASPED as a muddy figure walked into the shed.

'Stop screaming,' it said. 'It's just me!'

Janet put the towel-torch back on.

It was George!

Pam stopped screaming.

'Thanks for totally *abandoning* me out there!' puffed George.

Peter ran over and put his arm round George and helped him on to one of the upturned flowerpots. He looked exhausted.

'Are you OK?' said Peter worriedly. 'I'm so sorry we left you behind! I, um, it was all such a rush. We didn't realise. I'm so sorry.'

Peter felt terrible. How could they not have noticed they were a man down? He blamed himself. He would definitely have to do headcounts from now on. He'd become far too slack lately. And this was exactly the type of thing that happened when you didn't follow all of the official Secret Seven Society rules.

'I fell off my bike,' panted George. 'Rolled down the hill. Climbed back up. But you were all gone. And Mr and Mrs Lockheart were there!'

'Did they see you?' asked Janet.

George shook his head. 'I hid and watched them. They were arguing and pointing down towards the tent. And then they stole my bike! I had to wait until I was sure they'd gone back down the hill and into the hotel before climbing up and running all the way back here.'

Jack threw George a towel and George began wiping himself down. He really was covered in mud.

'You must have been so scared!' said Pam. 'I'm so

sorry we didn't notice. We've been sitting in the dark because we thought the Lockhearts might still be following us.'

She didn't mention that actually they'd had a torch on and been speaking for the past ten minutes and that they still hadn't noticed George was missing.

'I was scared,' said George. 'Especially because the Lockhearts were being so weird.'

Janet moved her flowerpot closer to George. 'What do you mean they were being weird?'

George looked up at her. Even with everything that was going on Janet had to bite her lip to stop herself from laughing because George had the most perfect mud moustache. It even had curly bits going up the sides.

'They were talking weird,' he said. 'Like they were pretending to be Scottish or something.'

Janet and Peter looked at each other. But before either of them could say a word Colin jumped up and started waving his arms around.

'Oh, my goodness! That's it! They weren't pretending to be Scottish! They've been pretending to be American!'

Colin looked around and stared at everyone. 'They're great big *fakers*!'

'And *thieves*,' said George. 'They stole my bike!'

CHAPTER TWELVE

THE LOCKHEARTS' REVENGE

THE NEXT day, the Secret Seven met on the hill where the Lockhearts had stolen George's bike the night before.

'This is pointless,' said George. 'I can't believe that you don't believe me!'

Peter put his hand on George's shoulder. 'It's not that we don't believe you, George. We do. It's just, well, you know what Colin's like. He likes to be sure of all the facts and science before we think about sharing what we've found with the police.'

'I don't think us standing on a hill, pretending to be the Lockhearts is very scientific, do you?' said Pam, crossing her arms.

She wanted to go and interview her uncle with

Barbara, just like Peter had asked them to do, but Colin had said that everyone had to be here for the reconstruction.

Colin ignored all the moaning and hurried about, preparing his crime scene.

'Are you sure that this is exactly where the bike was?' he asked.

George nodded. 'Look, you can see the tyre marks in the mud there.'

Colin dropped to the ground to inspect them. He loved this kind of thing and wanted to be a police detective when he grew up.

'OK,' said Peter. 'Let's get started.'

Colin jumped up and wiped himself down. It was time to do the reconstruction.

'OK. George, I need you to roll down the hill again,' said Colin.

Jack burst out laughing.

George looked at Colin angrily. 'No!' he said. 'I'll hide in the exact spot I hid in last night. I don't need to actually roll down the hill and scramble back up again. I know exactly where I was because I was stuck there for ages. By *myself*!'

The rest of them looked at each other sheepishly.

Barbara huffed and sat down on the ground near George's hiding place and began throwing rocks.

'Stop messing with my crime scene!' said Colin.

'Explain to me why we're doing this again?' she said.

So Colin explained that they needed to eliminate doubt, which meant that they had to be scientifically a hundred per cent sure that George would have been able to hear the Lockhearts' accents clearly from where he'd been hiding because so far he was the only person who had both seen and heard the Lockhearts talking in Scottish accents.

'Fine,' said George. 'Let's get this over with.'

'Right, so, Janet, you'll be Mrs Lockheart. And Peter, you'll be Mr Lockheart,' said Colin. 'Now stand there, right beside the bike.'

'I'd really rather not pretend my brother is my husband,' said Janet.

Jack laughed.

'It's fine,' said Peter. 'Let's just get this done. What do you want us to do?'

Colin got out his measuring tape and measured the distance from George to Peter and Janet.

'Twenty metres exactly,' he said. 'OK, Peter and Janet, start arguing in your best Scottish accents.'

Jack took a bite of his apple and sat down. 'This should be good.'

'I don't think I can do a Scottish accent,' said Janet.

'Of course you can,' said Colin. 'You've been on holiday in Scotland for a fortnight! Just copy your gran's voice, OK? *Go!*'

Janet sighed and looked at Peter. 'What shall we argue about?'

'GEORGE!' Peter yelled. 'What EXACTLY did you hear them say?'

'I COULDN'T HEAR EVERYTHING!' George shouted back from where he was hiding. 'But Mr Lockheart kept telling Mrs Lockheart to "CALM DOWN" and Mrs Lockheart kept saying, "THIS IS ALL YOUR FAULT." She also called him quite a few curse words.'

Janet's eyes lit up.

'Don't even *think* about it,' said Peter. 'I'll tell Mum.'

Janet smiled.

'OK, go!' said Colin.

So Janet and Peter began fighting in what were probably the worst Scottish accents anyone had ever heard.

Jack laughed so much he had actual tears running down his face and Pam was doing the snorting thing she sometimes did when she laughed too much.

'Can we stop now?' said Peter. He was feeling seriously embarrassed.

'Wait. Let me check with George and Barbara

first,' said Colin as he rushed over to where they were hiding.

But when Colin got there he didn't even need to ask if they'd managed to hear Peter's and Janet's accents clearly because they were both rolling around with laughter and Barbara couldn't even stand up she was laughing so much.

'Remember when Peter tried to say "who"?' cried Barbara. 'He sounded like a baboon!'

'OK!' snapped Peter. 'That's enough.' He stormed off down the hill.

'PETER!' Jack yelled. 'Where are you going?'

'AYE, DINNAE BE LIKE THAT. WAIT FIR US!' shouted Barbara in an excellent Scottish accent.

'Wow. You're really good at that!' said Janet.

Barbara shrugged. 'Not as good at the Lockhearts, of course. I can't believe they've been pretending to be American.'

'It's probably not the only thing they're pretending about,' said Colin.

'Moving here to open a new hotel and restaurant is obviously just a cover.'

'It's a pretty rubbish cover,' said Barbara. 'It's a stupid idea to open a restaurant when they clearly have no idea how to cook.'

All of a sudden they heard Peter shouting.

Janet bolted down the hill, even though her ankle was still hurting a bit.

She stopped dead in her tracks when she saw what Peter was looking at.

It was George's bike. Or what was left of it.

'My bike!' cried George. 'It's broken!'

It was more than broken. The bike had been pulled apart and burnt.

'My mum's going to kill me!' cried George. 'I can't believe the Lockhearts did this!'

'Just because they were the last ones with the bike, we can't be sure it was them who set it on fire,' said Colin. 'We don't have the evidence to prove that.'

Janet looked over at the hotel. She wondered if

the Lockhearts were watching them right now. 'Well, I think it was them,' she said. 'It was probably a warning to *stay away*.'

CHAPTER THIRTEEN

THE PINEAPPLE UPSIDE-DOWN CAKE

THAT EVENING, Pam, Barbara and Jack went to visit Pam's uncle to interview him about the Lockhearts.

It was only supposed to be Pam and Barbara but Jack said that he lived close to Pam's uncle so he might as well come too, just in case Pam and Barbara needed any extra help with taking notes or anything else.

But everyone knew that the real reason Jack wanted to go was because Pam had said her uncle was an excellent cook and that Jack was probably hoping there would be a cake or pastry in it for him.

When they arrived at Pam's uncle's house, he invited them in and left them in the living room while he went to the kitchen to make some tea.

When he came back, he had a pot of tea and a small plate with three plain biscuits on it.

Jack was gutted. He'd been sure he'd smelt some sort of cake when he walked in. This was a pretty disappointing display for someone who was supposed to be a head chef.

'Will you not have a biscuit, Uncle Jim?' asked Pam, once her uncle had passed the plate around.

'No, I'm fine, love. Not had much of an appetite recently.'

Pam looked at her uncle. She was sure he'd lost weight.

'Are you OK for us to ask you a few questions for our investigation, Uncle Jim?'

Uncle Jim smiled. 'Of course. I've always time for my favourite niece and her band of detectives. It'll cheer me up, I'm sure.'

Pam opened her pad and flicked to the first question she'd prepared.

'Why did you get fired from the hotel before

you'd even started?'

Uncle Jim took a sip of his tea. 'Why are you so interested in my job at the hotel?' he asked.

'We're actually investigating the Lockhearts,' said Barbara in her most serious voice. 'We think they've been behaving a bit suspiciously and we'd like to keep a close eye on them.'

Uncle Jim let out a big laugh. 'Good! Happy to hear it. Pretty sure they deserve all of your attention. Serves them right.'

He got up and walked towards the kitchen again. 'I think I will have a biscuit after all. You've cheered me right up!'

A few moments later Uncle Jim appeared with a tin. He opened it and Jack gasped. It was a pineapple upside-down cake. Jack knew he'd smelt something delicious!

'Made this earlier to keep myself busy. Was going to try to sell it to the café this afternoon but I think you lot deserve it.'

Jack agreed and set about cutting the cake and dishing it out while Uncle Jim sat back down.

'Don't know what to tell you,' he said. 'I was hired by phone by the Lockhearts a few months ago. They asked me to work on the menus before they arrived in the UK, so that's what I did. And then before I even met them they phoned and sacked me!'

Uncle Jim shook his head and took a great big bite of the pineapple cake.

Pam wrote down everything her uncle had just said as quickly as she could. Her writing was a bit messy but she knew she could write it out again, neatly, after the interview before she showed Peter and the others.

'Rotten of them!' said Uncle Jim. 'I'd already given my notice in at the café and the pub. So there's no chance either of them will take me back.'

He put down his plate on the table and stared at it for a bit.

'And you know what the worst thing about it all

is? Mrs Lockheart never even gave me a reason. She actually hung up the phone before I could ask!'

'Did you try to call her back?' asked Pam.

Uncle Jim shook his head. 'No, no. I know when I'm not wanted.'

Pam could feel herself getting angry. Her uncle was probably one of the nicest people in the world and an excellent cook. The Lockhearts had no right to treat him this way.

'Don't worry, Uncle Jim,' she said. 'We're pretty sure they're up to something and the Secret Seven have no intention of letting them get away with it!'

Uncle Jim looked at the three of them. 'What exactly do you think they're up to?'

Pam thought for a minute. She knew that one of the rules of the Secret Seven was to keep their investigations a secret. Peter would not be pleased if she broke the rules.

'Let's just say we think they've got a few secrets,' said Pam as professionally as she could.

Pam's uncle nodded and took another bite of his cake.

'Did you notice anything at all suspicious about the telephone call?' asked Barbara.

Uncle Jim thought for a moment. 'Not that I can think of.'

'What about Mrs Lockheart's accent?' said Pam.

Uncle Jim looked confused. 'What do you mean?'

'Did she sound American or Scottish?' Jack asked.

'American, of course! That's where they're from. Washington, I think.'

'What about the other restaurant staff? Do you know if anyone else was fired?' asked Pam.

'Tim, my sous-chef, got the boot too,' said Uncle Jim, shaking his head. 'And I heard Mrs Chen's son got a similar phone call. He's worked there since last year, cleaning the rooms. Got a phone call a few hours before he was due in saying they no longer needed him. Marty down the road too. They sent him away when he turned up to cut the grass, I heard. He's been the gardener there for over thirty years. Can you believe it?'

Pam jotted everything down as fast as she could.

'Sounds like they sacked everyone who was meant to be working there!' said Barbara.

'Goodness only knows what they're up to. But they've put a lot of people around here out of work. Can't say they'll be very popular for that. Rotten thing to do, if you ask me.'

Pam thanked her uncle for the interview and said they'd better be going.

'I see. Suppose you've got another secret meeting to get to! Wait there. I'll wrap the rest of this cake up for you to take back for the others.'

Pam beamed. Her uncle's cake was absolutely delicious and now she'd be able to show everyone just how good a cook he was.

But then, just as they were leaving, Uncle Jim said, 'Oh. Not sure if this'll be helpful to you or not but I've just remembered there *was* something a bit strange about the phone call.'

Pam's eyes went wide.

'Mrs Lockheart said she was calling from the airport and that she had to be quick because her flight was due to take off any minute. But before she hung up I heard something a bit odd.'

'What, what did you hear?' asked Pam urgently.

'I heard loads of dogs howling and barking in the background. Sounded like she was in a dog pound! Didn't think all those dogs would be allowed in the airport.'

CHAPTER FOURTEEN

THE EVIDENCE

WHEN PAM, Barbara and Jack arrived at the shed, Peter wouldn't let them in.

'The password has been changed!' he shouted through the door. 'You've all been notified by post.'

Peter had decided that it was time to be stricter with the official Secret Seven Society rules since the whole George-being-left-behind thing. He didn't want anything like that to happen ever again. He'd started this society and it was up to him to keep everyone safe and that meant that no one got into the shed without saying the correct password and wearing their official Secret Seven badge.

'We haven't been home yet, Peter,' Jack said through the door. 'We came straight here from the interview!'

But Peter wouldn't budge.

'Well, you'll just have to go home and open your post and come back with the correct password. And make sure you're all wearing your badges too!'

'Oh, for goodness' sake!' said Jack, shaking his head and knocking on the shed door even louder. '*Peter!* Let us in!'

'Can we take a guess?' asked Barbara? 'Is it *Baboon*?'

Jack burst out laughing.

'Stop it!' said Pam. 'He'll never let us in! Peter, we have some *seriously important* information to share. We found out something suspicious during our interview.'

'We also have a rather large pineapple upside-down cake,' said Barbara.

Peter thought about all of that. Especially the cake.

'Do you all at least still remember the old password? And have your badges with you?'

'*Yes!*' said Jack.

'Scotland!' said Pam.

Peter reluctantly opened the door and made each of them show him their badge before letting them in.

Pam sliced up the cake right away and passed it around so everyone could see just how delicious it looked.

'Oh, wow!' said George. 'This might be the best cake I've ever eaten!'

'I told you he was good,' said Pam.

She set about fixing her notes and rewriting things while everyone enjoyed the cake. Then when she was ready she explained everything that her uncle had told them in the interview.

'So they've sacked everyone,' said Colin, wiping pineapple syrup from his face.

Pam nodded. 'That's why the restaurant is such a disaster. They obviously don't want anyone working there in case they find out what they're up to.'

'What about the dog thing?' asked George. 'Are

dogs even allowed in airports?'

'I think pets are allowed to travel in the cargo bit,' said Colin.

'But Pam's uncle said it sounded like there were loads of them in the background. That's a bit weird, isn't it?'

Peter wrote something down on his pad. 'I think Mrs Lockheart might have been lying,' he said without looking up. 'She might not have been in an airport or in America. She could have made the call from a park or something near here and this is all part of her pretending to be American.'

Everyone agreed that it was unlikely there would be lots of dogs in an airport all barking like Pam's uncle had said and that Mrs Lockheart might have lied.

'OK, this is where we are with the investigation,' said Peter, holding the pad up for everyone to see:

EVIDENCE

- Holes all over hotel grounds (hidden by a huge tent)
- Two skulls have been found in the hotel grounds, in or near holes
- The Lockhearts lied about the tent being for a wedding
- Opened a new restaurant but can't cook (receipt for frozen pies)
- Sacked all their staff
- Five members of the Secret Seven have heard the Lockhearts speaking with a Scottish accent
- The Lockhearts stole George's bike

CONCLUSIONS

- The Lockhearts are pretending to be American (fake accents), so they may well have lied about being at the airport when they called Pam's uncle
- When they stole George's bike, they set it on

fire as a warning to us to stay away
- Didn't want us looking upstairs in the hotel – probably where they're hiding whatever they've dug up
- Definitely dangerous

George studied the list of evidence closely.

'I think it's time to tell the police what we've found out,' he said.

Peter shook his head. 'Not yet. We need more evidence to see if our suspicions are correct. We need to find whatever they've been digging up. Then we'll have real proof.'

'But we could show them my bike!' said George.

Peter looked over towards the corner of the shed where they'd hidden George's burnt bike under an old blanket.

'The bike is evidence that someone isn't happy

with us, but we can't actually prove it was the Lockhearts who did it. And none of us saw them do it.'

George looked worried. He knew what Peter was about to say before he even said it.

'We have to go back,' said Peter. 'We need to search that hotel from top to bottom until we find out what they're hiding in there.'

George gulped. 'But – but what about what they did to my bike?' he said. 'It was a warning!'

'That's exactly why we need to go back,' said Janet. 'We can't let them get away with this.'

Pam thought of her uncle and how thin and upset he'd looked and about how he didn't have a job now because of what the Lockhearts had done to him.

'Janet's right,' said Pam, standing up. 'We can't let them get away with this. Let's *get them*!'

CHAPTER FIFTEEN

THE HORROR-MOVIE WORKSHOP

THE NEXT day, the Secret Seven spent a few hours making a plan and eating the delicious picnic lunch Peter and Janet's mum had made them. There were ham sandwiches cut into little triangles, little cubes of cheese, mini sausage rolls, ginger biscuits, homemade lemonade and freshly baked scones with jam, cream and butter.

'Mmmmm,' said Barbara. 'The scones are making the butter and jam all yummy and melty!'

'Your mum's amazing,' said Jack, cramming a ham sandwich and a sausage roll into his mouth at the same time.

By 3 p.m. the Secret Seven were absolutely stuffed and had a brilliant plan.

'It's a bit risky,' said George.

Peter nodded. It was risky. And a lot of it depended on Barbara's acting skills and Mrs Bagnell's old horror-movie make-up!

The plan was to check in to the hotel as a guest because Mr Lockheart had made it very clear that upstairs was for guests only.

They knew that they were too young to book a room by themselves, even if they could afford to pay for it with the money Janet had been given for her birthday from her gran. That's when Pam, Barbara and Janet had come up with a brilliant idea.

Pam and Barbara would dress up as old women.

Peter wasn't sure at first, but then Janet explained that Mrs Bagnell would help them. 'Who is Mrs Bagnell?' asked Peter.

'Do you not remember her, Peter? She does stage make-up and makes masks and fake heads for horror movies. She helped with our school play last year.'

'But what if Mrs Bagnell says we can't borrow

her stuff?' asked George.

'Don't worry,' said Janet. 'I'm sure she will. She was really helpful and kind when we met her. She even taught me how to do the fake skin. It was pretty cool.'

'I remember!' said Jack. 'Barbara looked *terrifying*!'

Barbara laughed. 'I was supposed to look terrifying. I was the troll under the bridge.' Barbara started doing her troll voice and wandering around the shed with her hair swinging over her face.

Everyone burst out laughing.

'Stop it!' cried Jack. 'I've eaten too much. I'm going to be sick!'

But Barbara wouldn't stop. She started climbing all over Jack and pretending to eat him. But then Jack went a bit pale and Barbara didn't want to get thrown up on so she stopped.

'Well,' said Colin, 'we obviously don't have to worry about Barbara being able to fake her voice. She's a pro!'

Barbara took a bow and did a twirly thing with her hand and pretended to accept a fake bouquet of flowers Pam handed to her. Then she sat down and said, 'My name is Agnes Pennyworthwinklehump and I am eighty years young.'

George actually gasped. That's how convincing Barbara sounded.

'You sound exactly like my gran!' said George. 'Unbelievable!'

Barbara winked. 'It's a skill and a curse. Now that you know my talents you'll have me doing all sorts of things for you. Like pretending to be your mum and phoning the school to say the dog ate your homework, for example.'

Jack sat up straight. 'Could you really do that? Because I've got this history assignment that I'm supposed to be doing over the summer and—'

'Forget it,' Barbara interrupted. 'I only use my powers for good.'

'About your name, Mrs Penny— Um . . . what

was it again?' asked Peter.

Barbara wrapped her cardigan over her head like a shawl. 'It's Mrs Pennyworthwinklehump the third, dear.'

'I see,' said Peter. 'Well, I think you might want to choose a name that's a little more believable, don't you? I mean, we're already pushing it by dressing you up as an eighty-year-old woman. I don't think you should have a ridiculous name too!'

'How dare you, young man!' said Barbara, going off into another one of her theatrical performances.

Peter rolled his eyes. He was starting to worry that Barbara wasn't taking this as seriously as she should be. If the Lockhearts found out she was one of the Secret Seven, she could be in serious danger.

'*Fine*,' Barbara eventually said. 'You can call me Mrs Pennyworth.'

Peter nodded and wrote the name down in his pad so he wouldn't forget.

Janet clapped her hands together and stood up.

'Right! Do we have any pineapple upside-down cake left?' she asked.

Pam checked in the tin. 'One slice,' she said.

'Perfect,' said Janet. 'We can take it with us. Let's go and pay Mrs Bagnell a visit.'

Mrs Bagnell was a little surprised to see seven children on her doorstep when she answered the door.

'Oh, hello!' she said. 'Can I help you?'

'Hello, Mrs Bagnell,' said Janet. 'Do you remember me? I'm Janet. You came to our school last year to help with the make-up for our school play. And this is Barbara – you made her into a terrifying troll!'

'Oh, yes, of course!' said Mrs Bagnell.

'Well, this is my brother and our friends. We're the Secret Seven,' said Janet, 'and we need your help.'

The Seven showed Mrs Bagnell their official S.S. badges.

Mrs Bagnell looked a bit surprised.

'We brought you some pineapple upside-down cake,' said Jack.

'It's made by one of the best chefs in the country!' Pam added.

Mrs Bagnell smiled. 'Well,' she whispered, 'I wasn't expecting a visit from a secret society this afternoon, but I enjoy being surprised! Would you like to come in? I hope I can find a space for all of you.'

Janet nodded and the Secret Seven went inside.

Janet had known before they left the shed that seven was probably too many people to visit Mrs Bagnell, but everyone had been dying to come because they knew there would probably be old horror-movie props lying around and fake blood and Dracula costumes and werewolf heads.

'Why don't I take you to my workshop?' said Mrs Bagnell. 'There's more space in there.'

Jack started jumping up and down. '*Yes!* This is it!' he said to Peter. 'It's going to be *brilliant*!'

And it was brilliant. Mrs Bagnell led them out of the kitchen door and down to a large workshop at the bottom of her garden.

Once inside, the Secret Seven didn't say a word for about ten minutes. They just wandered around, looking at all the costumes and props with their mouths wide open.

'I'm semi-retired now. But I still like to do the odd piece if I'm asked. This is what I'm working on at the moment,' she said, pointing to a waxy ball sitting on a large desk. She turned the ball round and everyone gasped.

'It's going to be my scariest monster head yet!' she said, grinning.

'Will it be used in a movie?' Colin asked eagerly.

'Oh, yes,' said Mrs Bagnell. 'Most of what you see here has been used in the big Hollywood horror movies.'

'*Wow*,' said Colin, picking up a hand and inspecting the fake veins closely.

'Did you make all of this yourself?' asked Peter.

'Most of it,' said Mrs Bagnell. 'I sometimes get other people to help me out with bits and pieces I can't quite do myself.'

'This place is *amazing*!' said Barbara and Pam, flicking through all the costumes. 'Can we try one on?' Pam asked excitedly.

'Help yourselves,' said Mrs Bagnell. 'That's my fancy-dress section. I rent them out for costume parties. There's a small changing curtain just over there in that corner.

'So, how can I help this secret society of yours?'

'Well,' said Barbara, 'maybe we could show you!'

Pam and Barbara picked out a few bits and pieces and went behind the curtain to get changed.

When they pulled the curtain back, they were both dressed as old women. Pam had a grey wig on and was wearing a cardigan draped over her shoulders and Barbara had a long flowery dress on with a shawl over her head.

Mrs Bagnell smiled. 'Let me guess. You'd like me to help make you look a little older than you are?' she asked.

'Well, that would be just lovely of you, my dear. If it's not too much trouble,' said Barbara in her eighty-year-old-woman voice.

Mrs Bagnell stared at Barbara for a moment and then she clapped her hands and gave a loud laugh.

'Wow! Now *that's* a talent!' she said. 'And I should know – I've been around my share of voice actors over the years. This one's destined for the bright lights of Hollywood, I'm sure of it!'

Barbara grinned.

'I assume this isn't for a school play,' said Mrs Bagnell, giving Janet a little smile.

'Um, well, no,' said Janet. 'I'm afraid it's a secret.'

Janet was worried that Mrs Bagnell wouldn't help them if she refused to tell her what it was for. But she was also pretty sure that Mrs Bagnell definitely wouldn't help them if she did tell her.

'I understand completely,' said Mrs Bagnell, giving Janet a wink. 'It's a *secret* society after all. Just promise me you won't try to sneak in to see a horror movie dressed like that. They give those films age ratings for a reason, you know.'

Janet promised that they wouldn't.

'OK!' said Mrs Bagnell as she began pulling out tubs of wax and paint and brushes. 'Let's get you both seats over here and I'll start preparing the face moulds.'

'Can we help?' asked Jack excitedly.

'Certainly. Janet here can show you how to prepare the mix for the mould, if you can still remember how to do that?'

Janet nodded enthusiastically that she did. Making a mould of Barbara's face had been one of the coolest things she'd ever done when Mrs Bagnell had let her help do it for the play.

'Can we borrow these costumes too, please?' asked Pam in her most polite voice.

'Of course you can,' said Mrs Bagnell. 'And I think I've got another grey wig somewhere around here. I'll look that out for you too. And a walking stick.'

Peter grinned. This was all coming together nicely.

He was starting to believe that they might just be able to pull this off!

CHAPTER SIXTEEN

PAM AND BARBARA IN DISGUISE

PAM AND BARBARA got quite a few looks when they were riding their bikes to the hotel.

'SLOW DOWN!' yelled Peter. 'It's not normal for eighty-year-olds to be able to ride bikes that fast. People are STARING!'

Jack laughed. 'And eighty-year-olds definitely can't do wheelies!'

Barbara stopped her bike. 'That's a very *ageist* thing to say, Jack. I bet there are some old people who can do wheelies you know. And I bet some could even ride their bikes faster than *you*!'

'OK,' said Janet. 'Let's stay focused. We're almost there.'

She let go of the handlebar and tapped her pocket

just to make sure the envelope with all her money was still in there. She didn't really want to spend all her savings on a hotel room for the night that they weren't even going to stay in but she knew it was vital to the investigation. She'd also decided that when she got home she was going to make Peter split his savings with her. That seemed only fair.

'OK, stop,' said Peter. 'This is as far as we can go without risking them seeing us all together.'

Pam and Barbara stashed their bikes in a bush and adjusted their wigs, glasses and tights.

'I just can't believe how *real* the wrinkly skin looks,' said Jack, reaching out to touch Barbara's face. 'It's amazing!'

Everyone stared at Pam and Barbara for a minute. They really did look amazing. Mrs Bagnell had done an excellent job.

'Remember to let Barbara do all the talking,' Janet said to Pam as she handed over the money.

Pam nodded and pretended to padlock her lips and throw away the key.

Peter gave Janet a look that she knew meant Peter was wondering if Pam was actually going to manage not to say anything.

Everyone watched as Pam and Barbara began hobbling down the road, arm in arm, towards the hotel.

'What if this doesn't work?' said Jack.

Just then Barbara dropped her walking stick. Janet watched as Pam crouched over really slowly and picked up the walking stick and gave it back to Barbara. Then she patted Barbara's hunched back before they both started to hobble down the road again.

Janet smiled. They were brilliant actors.

'Don't worry,' she said. 'It'll work.'

As soon as Pam and Barbara stepped inside the hotel, Pam started to panic.

'It's OK, my dear,' said Barbara in her old-lady voice, 'we're here now. Soon you'll be able to have a lie-down.'

Barbara squeezed Pam's hand and gave her a look. Pam relaxed. She knew she didn't have to say anything. All she had to do was stand there and look old. Barbara would do the rest. It was going to be fine.

There was no one at the check-in desk so Barbara reached up and gave the bell a ding. That's when she caught sight of her hand. It looked far too young to belong to an eighty-year-old!

Barbara gasped and quickly pulled her hand back and tucked it inside her cardigan pocket. She hadn't thought to ask Mrs Bagnell to put some of the fake skin on her hands. She'd have to keep them hidden.

Just then someone came rushing down the stairs. Barbara quickly whispered to Pam about keeping her hands tucked away.

'Hey there!' said Mrs Lockheart in her fake

American accent. 'How can I help you ladies?'

That's when Barbara decided to go against the plan. She wasn't just going to do an old-lady voice. She was going to do a Scottish old-lady voice. She knew that Mrs Lockheart was Scottish and she wanted to see if hearing another Scottish accent would spook her.

'Hello there, lass. My name's Mrs Pennyworth. My sister and I would like a wee room for the night, please.'

It worked. Mrs Lockheart got a strange look on her face.

'Oh. Well, I'm sorry but we're fully booked for tonight.'

Pam started to panic a little. They hadn't discussed what to do if this happened!

Barbara made a decision there and then that she wasn't leaving until Mrs Lockheart found them a room. She wasn't wearing a wax face mask and itchy old-lady tights for nothing!

'Och, is there nothing you can do, lass? We've travelled all the way doon fae Glasgow! A tiny wee room would be fine. We dinnae take up much space.'

But Mrs Lockheart wouldn't budge.

'I'm sorry. We're absolutely packed. We're hosting a wedding this evening.'

Barbara knew she was lying about the wedding, which probably meant she was lying about the hotel being fully booked too.

Suddenly Pam collapsed to the ground.

Barbara gasped and was just about to scream in her normal voice when she realised what Pam was doing. She was acting!

Barbara watched as Pam shook her head and pointed to her hip.

'Oh, no,' said Barbara. 'She's got a terrible hip. She's been up tae high doh with it this week, I'll tell you! It's been like that since the war.'

Mrs Lockheart picked up the phone. 'I'll call an ambulance.'

'No, no. No need for that! She just needs a wee lie-down, don't you, Betty?'

Just then Mr Lockheart appeared and rushed over to Pam. 'What's happened? Is she *dead*?' he asked in a Scottish accent.

Mrs Lockheart's eyes went wide. She cleared her throat loudly.

'No, she just needs a bed for the night,' said Barbara. 'Poor lamb's got a bad hip and has just taken a wee tumble, that's all. Completely exhausted she is.'

'Let me help you up, miss. You can have a lie-down upstairs in one of our guest rooms,' said Mr Lockheart in a terrible American accent.

Mrs Lockheart looked furious. 'But we're fully booked! We have the wedding this evening, *remember*?'

'It's fine,' said Mr Lockheart. 'I'm sure I can find one room for the night.'

He helped Pam to her feet. 'There's a room on the

first floor that's free. It's only a few stairs. I hope that's OK?' he said.

'That'll be fine,' said Barbara. 'She'll feel much better after a wee lie-down, won't you, Betty?'

Pam nodded and gave a little smile.

As soon as Mr Lockheart left them alone in their hotel room, Pam began jumping up and down.

'WE DID IT!' she cried. 'We really did it!'

Barbara giggled. 'Shhhhh!'

'Oops. Sorry!' said Pam, covering her mouth.

They both stood there, grinning from ear to ear.

'You were brilliant,' said Barbara. 'That was genius!'

Pam leapt on to the bed and began jumping up and down again.

She laughed. 'That was so much fun. I thought it was going to be terrifying but it wasn't at all. It was *exciting*!'

Barbara climbed up on to the bed with Pam and

they both jumped up and down until they caught sight of themselves in the mirror and burst out laughing.

'*Oh!*' said Barbara. She'd completely forgotten. 'We'd better give Peter and the others the signal.'

Pam leapt off the bed and rummaged around in her old-lady handbag for the binoculars they'd brought from the shed.

'Good thing they've put us in a room looking out the back,' said Barbara.

Pam and Barbara looked out of the window. The tent was directly below them.

Pam looked through the binoculars. 'I can see them!' she said excitedly. 'There on top of the hill!'

Barbara reached into her own old-lady handbag and pulled out a red scarf. 'I hope this works,' she said.

Pam lifted up the window and Barbara reached her arm out and waved the scarf backwards and forwards to signal to the others that they were in.

Pam looked through the binoculars again. Peter was waving back. So was Jack. And Colin was jumping up and down with excitement.

'Right,' said Barbara. 'Time to start snooping around!'

Pam nodded and adjusted her wig.

'Ready?' said Barbara.

Pam nodded again. And they both threw their handbags over their shoulders and walked out of the room into the corridor.

CHAPTER SEVENTEEN

AN EXCITING DISCOVERY!

THERE WERE another five rooms in the corridor.

'OK,' said Barbara. 'We're going to start at the far end and listen outside the rooms and, if there's no noise coming from inside, we're going to try the door handles, OK?'

Barbara could see that Pam was nervous. 'Don't worry,' she said. 'If we get caught, we'll just say we forgot which room was ours, OK?'

Pam nodded and relaxed a bit. She kept forgetting they were in disguise.

Pam and Barbara made their way down the corridor, listening carefully outside each of the hotel room doors before trying them. But they were all locked.

'Look!' said Pam. 'The last room: 101. Isn't that the room Peter and Jack mentioned they got caught trying to search?'

Barbara nodded and reached forward slowly to turn the handle.

Pam grabbed her hand to stop her. 'Listen!' she hissed. There were voices coming from inside. Scottish voices!

They looked at each other. This must be the Lockhearts' room.

Pam and Barbara put their ears up to the door. Pam could hardly hear because her heart was pounding so hard.

'What were you *thinking*?' they heard Mrs Lockheart say.

'We only had one more guest to get rid of and the hotel would've been completely empty so we could get on with it. Now we have another two guests!'

'Calm down,' said Mr Lockheart. 'They'll be gone in the morning. What would you rather I'd done? Call an ambulance and risk having people asking questions about what happened here and why we couldn't let an old lady lie down? We're talking about a couple of old ladies! They won't hear a thing.'

Mrs Lockheart scoffed. 'Won't hear a thing?' she cried. 'You'd better hope not. You've only gone and put them in a room overlooking the tent!'

'I didn't realise at the time,' said Mr Lockheart. 'I was trying to keep them as far away from *you-know-what* as possible. Look,' he continued, 'even if they do see something, what are they going to do about it, eh? They're just a couple of old wifies.'

Pam and Barbara looked at each other and smiled.

The Lockhearts had no idea who they were dealing with.

They were the Secret Seven!

Pam and Barbara made their way down the staircase, through the restaurant and into the kitchen as planned. Since all the hotel bedrooms were locked, they decided to start snooping in the kitchen.

'Did you hear what Mrs Lockheart said about getting rid of all the guests so they could "get on with it"?' Pam whispered as they walked through the empty restaurant. 'She means the digging, doesn't she? I bet the holes are metres deep under that tent by now.'

Barbara nodded. 'And did you hear what Mr Lockheart said about wanting to keep us away from "you-know-what"? He obviously meant whatever they've been digging up, didn't he?'

Pam nodded back. 'We need to find out what it is!'

Pam and Barbara sneaked into the restaurant kitchen and began opening all the cupboards and drawers and looking inside. But there was nothing there except brand-new cutlery and pots and pans that looked like they'd never been used.

'Over there!' whispered Barbara, pointing to a

small room to the side of the kitchen.

It was the pantry.

'See,' said Pam, 'if there really was a wedding going on here tonight, there would be loads of food in here. But there's hardly anything!'

Barbara and Pam looked around and peeked inside boxes. There was nothing except a few cans of beans and more unused kitchen supplies. The Lockhearts didn't seem to be hiding anything here.

'What about in there?' said Pam, pointing to a big freezer at the back of the room.

Barbara walked over and lifted the freezer lid up.

Pam closed her eyes. She was a bit scared to look in case it was full of Ancient Roman skeletons.

'Oh, wow! *Look!*' said Barbara.

Pam opened her eyes and saw something she wasn't expecting. Money. A lot of money.

Barbara leant in and pulled out a plastic bag full of notes and stared at it with her mouth wide open.

'I bet it's stolen!' whispered Pam.

Pam and Barbara both stared at the bag of money. There must have been thousands of pounds in there!

Then Pam spotted something else.

She leant into the freezer and pulled out a small see-through plastic bag with two purple rectangles inside.

'What are those?' asked Barbara.

Pam opened the bag. 'I think they're passports,' she said.

She pulled one out. It was definitely a passport. She flicked through the pages until she reached the photo page.

'Look!' she whispered, showing Barbara the photo. 'They've been using fake names!'

Barbara looked at the passports. The photos were definitely of Mr and Mrs Lockheart. But the names said Mr and Mrs Brown. The passports also weren't American ones – just as the Seven had suspected.

Barbara gasped. 'This is serious evidence! Put them in your handbag!'

AN EXCITING DISCOVERY!

'But what if they notice they're gone?' said Pam.

'Well, hopefully the police will be here by then to arrest them. Plus, if we leave them here, they might use them to escape with all the cash!'

Pam put the passports in her handbag and closed the freezer lid and they both rushed out of the pantry and back into the kitchen.

But they weren't alone.

CHAPTER EIGHTEEN

THE SCRATCHING NIGHT GHOST

'WHAT ARE you doing here?' said an angry voice.

Pam gripped Barbara's hand and they spun round to see Mr Lockheart at the back door.

'Oh, hello again, young man,' said Barbara. 'I think we're a bit lost. Looking for the restaurant. Could you be a dear and help us?'

The man narrowed his eyes at them. 'Restaurant's closed,' he said.

'Oh, that's a shame,' said Barbara. 'My sister and I were just looking for a wee cup of tea and a biscuit, weren't we, Betty?'

'You should go back to your room,' he said. 'There's a kettle in there.'

'Oh. We didn't realise. What silly old dears we

are. Well, it was nice to talk to you.'

The man watched as Pam and Barbara hobbled out of the kitchen as quickly as they could.

'Phew, that was close! Let's get back to the room and wait for the others to get here,' whispered Barbara as they headed back through the restaurant.

But when they reached the reception desk they saw a man in a suit standing there. He was arguing with Mrs Lockheart.

The man had a suitcase with him and he did not look pleased.

'Well, I'm not staying in that room another night!' he said angrily.

'I was up half the night with all the noise coming from above. It sounded like scratching! What exactly is going on up there?'

Pam stared at Barbara.

'There's *nothing* going on up there!' said Mrs Lockheart, getting a bit flustered. 'The top floor is completely empty and *out of bounds*. We've had some flooding. It must be the hotel ghost you heard.'

The man rolled his eyes.

'I don't know what to tell you, sir. We simply don't have any other rooms available. But we can give you a full refund for your entire stay if you leave. Now.'

Pam and Barbara looked at each other. This must be the only other guest in the hotel that they'd overheard Mr and Mrs Lockheart talking about.

Barbara wondered what he'd heard and what exactly was going on up on the top floor. They had to find out.

She had an idea. 'Excuse me, young man,' said Barbara, hobbling forward. 'I'm Mrs Pennyworth. We'd be happy to switch rooms with you. You can take our room on the first floor. We're mostly deaf, you see. A little night ghost won't bother us one bit. In fact, I doubt we'll hear a thing.'

The man smiled and looked back at Mrs

Lockheart. 'There you go,' he said. 'Problem solved thanks to these ladies.'

The man walked over to Barbara and put out his hand to shake hers. 'I'm Mr Dhar,' he said. 'Thank you very much for your kindness.'

Barbara hesitated. She didn't want anyone to see her young person's hand!

'Och. You can give me a wee peck on the cheek,' she said. 'Lovely young man like you!'

The man laughed and bent down and gave Barbara a quick kiss on the cheek.

Pam smiled. She was so proud of how well Barbara was managing to trick everyone. She was proud of herself too. She couldn't wait to tell the others what a brilliant job they'd done.

'Let me come and help you with your bags,' said Mr Dhar. 'Then I'll take you up to the room.'

'What about all those stairs?' Mrs Lockheart protested.

It was obvious that she wanted Mr Dhar to leave.

Then she'd only have two old ladies to worry about.

'Oh, we'll be fine,' said Barbara. 'Betty here needs the exercise. Can't let that hip of hers seize up again.'

Mrs Lockheart glared at them. Her face was bright red.

Mr Dhar chatted away to Pam and Barbara on their way to the room about how he was here on a business trip and the trouble he'd had trying to check in and the noises coming from above in the night and how the hotel food was shocking.

'I'm checking out first thing tomorrow morning,' he said. 'I can't wait to get out of here!'

When they reached Pam and Barbara's room, Barbara asked him to wait outside while they gathered their stuff. They didn't really have anything other than a small empty bag that they'd brought just to make it look like they had luggage.

'Grab the binoculars!' whispered Barbara. 'I'll tidy up the bed.'

Once they were packed, Mr Dhar led them up

the stairs to the third floor and along the corridor to their new room.

'There you go,' he said, handing them his keys.

'Don't you need anything from inside?' asked Barbara.

The man pointed to the suitcase in his hand. 'Nope. All packed,' he said. 'Like I said to Mrs Lockheart, I couldn't spend another night in that room. Thank you both so much for swapping with me. I've got an important business meeting early in the morning so I need at least one good night's sleep!'

Mr Dhar said goodbye and Barbara opened the door and went inside.

'OK. The new plan is to focus on searching the top floor,' said Barbara. 'There's obviously something up there that the Lockhearts, or should I say *the Browns*, don't want anyone to know about.'

'Wait,' said Pam. 'What if the hotel *is* haunted? I don't want to see the Scratching Night Ghost!'

'Don't worry,' said Barbara, pulling Pam inside and shutting the door. 'Mrs Lockheart was probably just making that up.'

Pam shuddered. She wasn't so sure. Plus, there was something odd about this room. It seemed a lot darker than their other room.

That's when she realised what was different. The window! It faced out in the opposite direction from their first room.

'Oh, no! We can't see out the back any more,' said Pam. 'We're facing the street! What are we going to do?'

'We'll just have to find another way to give Peter the signal that they should come and help us search the hotel,' said Barbara. 'Come on. Follow me!'

CHAPTER NINETEEN

TIME FOR BACKUP

LUCKILY ONE of the windows on the staircase looked out over the hotel grounds and towards the hill.

Barbara made sure no one was looking and then she opened the window and waved the red scarf.

'I think it's getting too dark for them to see us,' said Pam.

Barbara looked at her watch. It was much later than she'd realised. It was almost 9.30 p.m! They must've spent more time at Mrs Bagnell's house than she'd thought.

Just then Pam's stomach made a loud grumbling sound. 'Sorry!' she whispered. 'I'm starving!'

Janet had said she'd let Barbara and Pam's mums know that they were having dinner at her house that night so they didn't worry when Pam and Barbara didn't come home to eat. But they hadn't thought to actually bring food to the hotel with them for their dinner.

'I think we need to use the torch,' said Pam.

'Good idea,' said Barbara.

She took the torch out of her handbag and flashed it out of the window three times and waited.

After a few seconds a light flashed back at them.

'It's them!' whispered Pam.

Pam and Barbara closed the window and sneaked downstairs and out of the front door of the hotel.

Five minutes later they heard bike brakes and rustling in the bushes.

Then a face poked out of the bushes. It was Jack.

Pam and Barbara waved and Jack came out of a bush followed by Peter.

'How's it going in there?' asked Peter.

'It's going brilliantly!' said Pam. 'We found

out loads. We're almost ready to go and get the police inspector.'

Peter looked surprised. Pam knew it was because he didn't realise how good she and Barbara actually were at investigating.

'So what now?' asked Jack.

'We need to search the top floor,' said Barbara.

She quickly explained that they'd overheard the Lockhearts talking about getting rid of the hotel guests so could 'get on with it' and how they'd been trying to keep them away from 'you-know-what'. Then Pam told them about the money and the passports and the false names and about the noises coming from the top floor.

Peter and Jack looked at each other.

They were stunned.

'I can't believe you took their passports,' said Jack. 'That's genius! Now they can't leave the country!'

Peter agreed. 'Well done for discovering their

real identities. You've done a brilliant job.'

Pam and Barbara smiled at each other.

'And there's definitely someone up on the top floor,' said Jack. 'We've been waiting on the hill for ages for your signal. When it started to get dark, we noticed that all the lights were off except for two rooms on the first floor and one on the top floor.'

Peter nodded. 'We almost didn't notice the light on the top floor until we looked through the binoculars and saw a small sliver of light coming from one of the windows. It looks like it's been boarded up. But there was definitely a light on in there.'

'Wait, did you say Mr Dhar heard scratching coming from up there?' asked Jack.

Barbara nodded.

'That's a bit weird, isn't it?' said Jack.

Pam shivered. She still wasn't absolutely sure there wasn't a Scratching Night Ghost.

Just then Janet and Colin peeked out of the bush. 'What's going on?' hissed Janet.

Peter turned and gave them the signal to stay where they were.

Janet scowled and disappeared back inside the bush.

'Right, we need to split up and search the rest of the hotel until we find out what they're hiding and then we'll go and get the police.'

'Shouldn't we just check the top floor?' asked Jack.

'No. We can't be absolutely sure that's where they're hiding something. We need to split up and have someone check their bedroom too.'

'That's probably Room 101. We heard them in there earlier. But it'll be locked,' said Pam.

'I'm guessing the rooms on the top floor will be locked too,' said Peter. 'That's why one of us is going to have to steal their keys!'

* * *

Jack knew Peter was going to ask him to be the one to sneak behind the reception desk and steal the keys. Peter always gave him the riskiest jobs to do.

Peter said it was because he trusted Jack the most but Jack wasn't so sure. He suspected Peter might sometimes ask him to do the risky stuff because he didn't want to do it himself.

Jack hid behind the big pillar at the front of the hotel while Pam and Barbara went up to the reception desk and asked Mrs Lockheart if she could help them find the downstairs toilet.

Mrs Lockheart sighed loudly and reluctantly led Pam and Barbara along the corridor. Once Jack was sure no one else was around, he ran behind the desk and began searching for the keys. But then he heard footsteps and even though he couldn't see who it was the footsteps sounded loud and he was sure it must be Mr Lockheart. If Mr Lockheart came behind the reception desk, he would be in big trouble!

Jack desperately looked around for somewhere to hide and spotted a small cupboard filled with paper and envelopes. It was pretty small but he didn't really have a choice. He pulled out the boxes of paper and squeezed himself inside and held the door shut.

Jack held his breath until he heard the footsteps disappear past him and up the staircase. Then he squeezed back out and began searching for the keys again until he eventually found them on a little hook inside another cupboard.

He peeked up over the desk to make sure no one was around and then leapt out and ran back to the bush where the others were waiting.

Jack dived through the bush and landed right on top of Peter.

'Ouch!' cried Peter.

'Sorry!' Jack puffed. 'Didn't get the keys. Almost got caught. Had to make a run for it.'

Peter looked panicked.

But then Jack grinned and dangled the keys in front of his face and Peter rolled his eyes and smiled.

'I've just finished telling the others everything Barbara and Pam found out,' said Peter. 'We've made a plan.'

The plan was that Pam and Barbara would keep a close eye on Mr and Mrs Lockheart and keep them as busy as possible so that the others could search their bedroom and the top floor.

Janet and George were going to search Room 101 and Peter and Jack were going straight up to the top floor.

If anyone was caught, they were to tell the Lockhearts that they were Mrs Pennyworth's grandkids and they were just looking for their gran's room.

Colin and Scamper were to stay in the bush outside and run to get the police if any of the others gave the signal that things had gone wrong.

George had wanted to be the one to stay in the

bush because he was mega scared but he wasn't as fast as Colin was so Janet convinced him to come with her.

Jack separated the keys and gave Janet and George the key to Room 101.

'Give us the key that says basement,' said Janet. 'We'll check there too. Just in case.'

Peter nodded. That was a good idea. A basement was a good place to hide things.

George groaned. He didn't like basements. He didn't like them at all.

'OK,' said Peter. 'This is it. Are we ready?'

Peter, Jack, Janet, George and Colin all looked at each other and nodded.

Peter smiled. 'Good. Then let's go, Secret Seven. We can *do this*!'

CHAPTER TWENTY

INSIDE ROOM 101

JANET AND GEORGE stood outside Room 101 and listened at the door. They knew Mrs Lockheart was downstairs but they needed to be sure Mr Lockheart wasn't in there.

After a few moments Janet gave George a nod and put the key in the lock and peeked inside. The room was empty. And a complete mess! There were clothes, newspapers and empty takeaway containers everywhere.

'Where do we start?' asked George nervously.

'You do the wardrobe,' said Janet. 'I'll check all the drawers and under the bed.'

There was nothing but more newspapers and clothes under the bed.

'Any luck in the wardrobe?' asked Janet.

'Just a few coats and some muddy boots,' said George.

'OK, come and help me search the chest of drawers. You start at the bottom, I'll start at the top.'

George rummaged around in the drawers. 'What about this?' he said. 'They've not even opened any of them.'

He held out a pile of post tied with an elastic band.

Janet took the pile from George and began flicking through the letters. Every single one was sealed.

'Why wouldn't they open their letters?' she asked.

George shrugged. Janet kept flicking through until she came across a picture of a beach. It was a postcard.

She pulled it out and turned it over. The address was a bit smudged but she could still make out the message.

Dear Eloise,

We're having a fantastic vacation in France! I can't wait to come and visit you in England before we head back to the States. Mom and Dad say hello. I hope you and your mom and dad are enjoying your new life in England. I'm sure the hotel and new restaurant are doing really well. No one can resist your parents' awesome food. I miss you so much. I can't believe my best friend lives in England now! Promise me you'll come back to Washington to visit me at least once a year! High school is going to be so lame without you. I miss your dogs so much too. Hello, Ben! Hello, Daisy! Hello, Molly! Hello, Alfie!

Lots of love, **Adya**

Janet stared at George.

'The Lockhearts – or whatever their name is – have got a daughter?' said George. 'Where is she? We've never seen a girl here.'

Janet didn't say anything. Her mind was racing.

'The dogs,' she said eventually. 'Do you remember what Pam's uncle said about hearing lots of dogs in the background when Mrs Lockheart called him?'

George nodded. 'Do you think these were the dogs he heard? They might be keeping them up on the top floor. That would explain the strange noises and scratching Mr Dhar heard. She must've phoned Pam's uncle from up there.'

Something didn't feel right to Janet. 'Why would they keep their dogs up there?' she asked.

'Maybe they're guard dogs protecting whatever they're hiding up there,' said George.

Janet wasn't sure what to think. There was something weird about this. And where was their daughter?

Janet slipped the postcard into her backpack and quickly finished checking the rest of the drawers.

She was just about to search the bathroom

when she spotted that the light was on behind the closed door.

She grabbed George and covered his mouth with her hand. She didn't want him to do one of his loud gasps.

Janet raised her arm and pointed to the light coming from under the door. Two foot-shaped shadows had appeared.

Someone was in there.

Someone had been listening to them this whole time!

Janet froze. She felt like her feet were made of cement.

She could feel George shaking.

And then all of a sudden the bathroom handle slowly started to move.

CHAPTER TWENTY-ONE

IMPOSTERS

JANET AND GEORGE ran out of the room and down the stairs.

'Keep going!' said Janet when they got to the bottom.

Janet had hoped they'd be able to run out of the front door and hide in the bush, but Mrs Lockheart was standing at the entrance, looking out. Janet hoped the woman hadn't spotted Colin and Scamper hiding in the bushes.

'This way!' said George, pointing to a door without a sign.

They had no idea where the door led but they knew that they had to get out of there before Mrs Lockheart turned and saw them or Mr

Lockheart came running after them.

The door opened on to a small set of stairs leading downwards, which ended at another door.

'The basement!' whispered Janet. 'Come on!'

George gulped and followed Janet down the stairs.

Janet pulled the key out of her pocket and shoved it in the lock. But it wouldn't turn!

'Come on! Come on!' whimpered George, hopping up and down. 'We need to *hide*!'

'I'm *trying*,' said Janet.

Eventually the key turned in the lock with a loud thump and they rushed inside and closed the door behind them.

It was dark inside. Pitch-black.

Janet took her torch out of her backpack and switched it on. 'We should be safe here,' she said.

George wasn't so sure. But he didn't fancy going back up and coming face-to-face with Mr Lockheart.

Janet shone her torch around the room. There were boxes everywhere.

The boxes were all sealed and labelled. George and Janet wandered around, reading the labels.

'It's all their stuff,' said George. 'Clothes, books, furniture, everything.'

'They're obviously not planning to stay,' said Janet. She positioned her torch on a shelf so it cast a light on the nearest box, labelled PILLOWS, and plumped herself on top of it. An odd jingling sound came from the box.

'That doesn't sound like pillows,' said George. They looked at each other and started tearing open the box. 'There's something rattling around at the bottom.'

George began pulling out loads of pillows until he spotted something at the bottom of the box. 'Are those pound coins?' he asked.

Janet shone her torch inside the box. 'Oh, my goodness!' she said, and reached inside and grabbed a handful of the coins. She gasped. 'They're *gold coins*!'

George gulped. There weren't just coins in there. There were ancient-looking rings and bracelets too.

'The Lockhearts must've found buried treasure!' said George. 'My granddad said that people did that in Roman times, instead of using a safe or a bank, and that sometimes they'd get killed in battle and the treasure would just be left there buried under the ground. Lost for ever!'

'Right, that would explain why they've been digging all those holes,' said Janet. 'This is the evidence we needed. We need to get the police here now!'

They were just about to leave when Janet spotted the label on one of the smaller boxes by the stairs. It said PHOTO ALBUMS.

'Here, hold the torch,' she said, and she began opening the box.

'Something's bothering me about that postcard. I want to check something quickly.'

Janet pulled out an album that said THE

LOCKHEART FAMILY ALBUM and turned to the first photograph.

It was a picture of two people on their wedding day.

'Who are they?' asked George.

Janet wasn't sure. She flicked to another photo in the album and froze.

It was a picture of the same man and woman and a girl sitting under a Christmas tree with four dogs.

Janet couldn't believe it. Her heart was racing.

'Wait a minute,' said George. 'Four dogs – that's what the postcard mentioned!'

Janet nodded. 'And so the girl in this photo must be Eloise, the girl that the postcard was for!'

Janet pointed to the Christmas stockings hung up behind the family on the fireplace. There were seven of them.

'Mum, Dad, Eloise, Ben, Daisy, Molly and Alfie,' said Janet.

George was confused.

'George,' she said, pointing to the picture. 'I think these people are the *real Lockhearts*.'

George still looked confused.

'You mean . . . the people upstairs are pretending to be this family?' he said.

Janet nodded. 'This isn't even their hotel,' she said. 'They're *imposters*!'

Just then there was a loud noise. Janet didn't realise what it was at first but then she recognised the sound. It was the lock on the basement door!

'Did we just get locked in?' asked George, panicked.

Janet put her hand in her pocket. The key. She'd left it in the lock outside!

'And you can STAY DOWN THERE!' a voice shouted through the door.

George gasped. They'd been caught!

Janet ran up the stairs. 'Oh, thank GOODNESS you're here!' she yelled through the door. 'We're

Mrs Pennyworth's grandchildren. She's staying here. We got lost looking for the toilet. Can you let us out, please?'

The voice on the other side of the door laughed. It was Mrs Lockheart (the *fake* Mrs Lockheart).

'Nice try,' she said in her Scottish accent.

Janet felt her stomach drop. Mrs Lockheart wasn't even pretending to be American any more.

'We know you two were snooping around in our room,' she said. 'My husband heard everything you said. Think you can pull the wool over our eyes, eh? Well, you're sorely mistaken, lass. I know it was you lot poking around the tent the other night too. I thought I'd made it perfectly clear what would happen if you came trespassing on our land again! Well, now you can stay down there until we figure out what to do with you.'

Janet looked down at George. They were trapped.

They both listened as Mrs Lockheart walked off and left them there.

'Oh, no,' said Janet. 'I think I just blew Pam and Barbara's cover. We need to warn them!'

She sat down on the steps and tried to think.

George started feeling the walls until he felt a switch and turned it on. The basement filled with light.

He looked around. There had to be another way out of here.

'Look!' he said.

There was a small window up high near the ceiling.

'Use the boxes!' said Janet, jumping up.

Janet and George piled up the boxes to make a tower up to the window.

George climbed up and pushed the window open. 'I'll go first and then help you get out, OK?'

Janet nodded. 'Hurry! We need to get up to the top floor and warn Peter and the others before the Lockhearts find them.'

'Wait,' said George, half out of the window.

'If they're keeping the treasure in the basement, what's on the top floor?'

Just then they heard the key turn in the lock again.

Someone was coming for them!

'GO!' yelled Janet. '*GO!*'

CHAPTER TWENTY-TWO

THERE'S SOMETHING ON THE TOP FLOOR

JANET AND GEORGE ran to the bush where Colin and Scamper were waiting.

'Are you OK?' Colin asked Janet.

George looked at Janet. She seemed like she was in pain.

'I'm fine,' she said, rubbing her ankle. 'I just hurt my ankle again crawling out of the basement window.'

Colin looked confused.

'It's a *loooong* story,' said George.

Scamper crawled over and began licking Janet's ankle.

'Thanks, boy,' she said, stroking his soft head.

Then she remembered Mrs Lockheart standing at

the entrance of the hotel earlier.

'Scamper didn't bark or anything, did he?' she asked.

Colin shook his head. 'He's been as good as gold.'

George smiled. 'Speaking of *gold*.' He pulled five gold coins out of his pocket.

Colin gasped.

'I think they might be Roman coins,' said George.

Colin grabbed one and began inspecting it. 'I think they are!' he basically squealed. 'Your granddad must have been right about the village being built on top of an Ancient Roman one.' He stared at George and Janet with wide eyes. 'There might be more. These coins might be part of a buried *treasure hoard*! That's what they've been digging up!'

'Shhhhhh!' said Janet.

'We need to take them to the police inspector now and tell him what the Lockhearts have been up to,' said George.

'You mean the *imposters*,' said Janet.

Colin looked confused again but there wasn't time to explain everything right now.

'I'm going back in to warn Peter and the others,' said Janet, standing up. 'You two take Scamper and go and get the police.'

George looked at Janet's face when she tried to put weight on her ankle. She'd hurt it more than she was letting on.

'I'll go and warn Peter,' said George. 'Colin can go and get the police and you stay here with Scamper, OK?'

'No way,' said Janet. 'I'm coming with you. Colin, take Scamper with you and get the police here as soon as you can!'

Peter and Jack made their way slowly along the top floor, opening doors and searching for the room with the boarded-up window that they'd seen from outside. They'd been searching for almost twenty minutes but they hadn't found it yet.

That's when they heard something.

It sounded like howling!

'It's coming from the other end of the corridor,' said Jack. 'Let's go!'

Jack and Peter hurried along the corridor to the very last room.

The howling had stopped but Jack was sure he could hear something else.

'All right, Daisy, don't worry. I'll get you the biggest bowl of doggy treats ever the moment we get out of here.'

'Listen!' whispered Peter.

'It's a girl's voice – and it sounds as if she's talking to a dog,' said Jack.

Peter looked down at the lock. There was a padlock on the outside of the door. 'Look!' he said. 'Whoever's in there with the dog has been locked in!'

Jack took the master keys out of his pocket and began searching for a padlock key. But there wasn't one.

Suddenly they heard a voice from inside.

'Who's there?' the voice said. Jack looked at Peter. It was definitely a girl. She sounded American.

Jack took a risk. 'Hello?' he whispered through the door. 'Who are you?'

Jack heard footsteps walking towards the door and then a male voice said, 'Hello? Please help us!'

Jack looked at Peter. There were people trapped in there.

Just then George and Janet burst on to the top floor and hurried along the corridor towards them.

'We need to get out. *Now!*' cried George.

'We can't!' said Jack. 'There are people locked in this room!'

Janet gasped. 'Oh, my goodness. That's it! It must be the real Lockhearts!' she said. Peter and Jack looked confused so Janet quickly explained about the photo album they'd found in the basement.

'The police are on their way,' said George. 'Colin's gone to get them.'

But then all of a sudden Mr and Mrs Lockheart came thundering along the corridor towards them.

'You little *brats*!' spat Mrs Lockheart. 'You think you can stop *us*?'

Peter looked around. There was nowhere to go.

'Don't even *think* about trying to escape!' she said nastily, unlocking the padlock and throwing the door open.

Jack tried to get away but Mr Lockheart blocked his path. He really was a giant *hulk* of a man!

'Get in! All four of you! Or we'll THROW you in!' yelled Mrs Lockheart.

Peter looked inside. There was a family sitting on a bed. The girl looked a couple of years older than they were and she had a little dog on her lap. They seemed terrified.

'How long have you been holding this family

hostage?' demanded Peter. 'You won't get away with this, you know!'

Mrs Lockheart laughed. 'That's what you think. Now *get in*!'

Peter, Jack, Janet and George reluctantly stepped into the room.

'We know that you're *imposters!*' cried Janet.

'You've been keeping the real Lockhearts captive and pretending to be them so you could dig up the grounds until you found the treasure hoard you were searching for.'

George reached into his pocket and showed Peter and Jack the gold coins.

The fake Mrs Lockheart's face went pure red.

'GIVE ME THOSE!' she screamed, grabbing the coins. 'We'll be long gone by the time anyone finds you here!' She looked at the family cowering on the bed. 'And then you lot can have your precious hotel back. It's a dump anyway.'

'What about our dogs?' the girl whimpered.

'You said you'd give us back our dogs if we stayed quiet.'

'The cheek of you! You've been hiding one from us!' she yelled. 'And we've been feeding you, haven't we? Isn't that enough?'

The girl started to cry and her mum and dad both hugged her. They looked absolutely exhausted.

Peter knew that he had to keep the fake Mrs Lockheart talking so she and her husband didn't run off before the police arrived. He couldn't let them get away with this. They weren't just thieves, they were kidnappers.

'I hope you're not planning to run off anywhere too far way,' said Peter, smiling. 'Mr and Mrs BROWN!'

Mrs Brown gasped. 'How do you know our names?' she demanded.

Mr Brown's face went pale.

'Stan! Go and check the freezer. NOW!' she shouted.

Mr Brown disappeared.

The girl started to cry even harder.

'Don't worry,' said George. 'The police will be here soon.'

Mrs Brown's eyes went wide. 'You've called the *police*?' she screamed.

And then she ran.

CHAPTER TWENTY-THREE

SCAMPER SNIFFS OUT TROUBLE

'STAY WITH the Lockhearts,' said Peter to Janet and George.

'Wait!' said the real Mr Lockheart. 'You should stay here too, son. The cops are on their way.'

But Jack had already left so Peter ran after him.

Jack and Peter followed Mrs Brown down the stairs and along the first floor towards the staircase.

She was getting away!

At that moment one of the hotel doors opened and a man in his pyjamas stepped out.

It was Mr Dhar.

'STOP HER!' Peter yelled. 'She's a CRIMINAL!'

The man lunged forward and grabbed Mrs Brown.

'GET OFF ME!' she screamed.

Just then a police inspector came rushing up the stairs with Pam, Barbara, Colin and Scamper behind him. Meanwhile two more police officers came through the front door and started to search the hotel.

The police inspector looked at Mrs Brown. 'I hear you've been busy in the garden!' he said.

Mrs Brown scowled at him. 'I'm not saying a *word*!'

'Have it your way,' said the inspector. 'By the time we've finished we'll have more than enough evidence against you.'

Mrs Brown groaned and slumped to the floor.

Everyone watched as the inspector handcuffed Mrs Brown and an officer came and led her down the stairs and out of the hotel.

'Great work, Secret Seven!' said the police inspector, shaking everyone's hands. 'I've got officers in the basement now, looking for the treasure hoard.'

'There's also a kidnapping situation,' said Peter.

'The Browns have been keeping the real Lockhearts hostage in one of the rooms upstairs.'

The inspector looked shocked.

'Um . . . can someone tell me what's going on here, please?' said Mr Dhar, scratching his head.

Pam giggled. He looked funny standing there in his stripy pyjamas.

'Poor Mr Dhar,' said Barbara in her normal voice. 'Looks like you're not going to get a good night's sleep after all!'

Mr Dhar's eyes went wide when he heard Barbara's voice.

'Sorry we had to lie to you. We're not actually old ladies,' said Barbara, peeling off a strip of her fake skin. 'We're the Secret Seven.'

Mr Dhar rubbed his face. 'I think I need to lie down.'

'George and Janet are with the Lockheart family,' said Peter. 'I think they're OK, but it looks like they've had a rough time.'

The police inspector shook his head. 'I can't believe they've been held hostage in their own hotel. Thank goodness you lot figured this out before the imposters ran off. They might have left them trapped up there! I'd better go and check on them,' he said.

'Wait!' said Pam. 'There's another criminal still on the loose. Where's Mr Brown?'

'Quick, check the kitchen!' shouted Peter.

The police inspector rushed down the stairs and into the kitchen followed by Pam, Barbara, Colin, Jack, Peter and Scamper. There was no sign of Mr Brown and the money was still in the freezer.

'We've got officers surrounding the hotel. He can't have got far.'

Then Barbara had a bright idea. 'What if he's hiding in the tent?'

They all raced round the back of the hotel.

The padlock had been removed but the tent was empty.

The inspector shone his torch around the tent. 'Would you look at all of these holes!' he said. 'Unbelievable what they've been up to.'

'He must've got away,' said Peter, disappointed.

'Don't worry, son,' said the police inspector. 'He'll be on foot. We'll find him.'

As they turned to leave, Scamper started growling.

'What's wrong, boy?' asked Peter. 'There's nothing here, Scamper. We've checked.'

Suddenly Scamper lunged forward and the lead slipped out of Peter's hand. Scamper began sniffing around the holes.

'He's probably looking for another bone,' said Jack.

But then Scamper stopped dead and began growling really loudly.

The police inspector walked over and peered into the hole Scamper was growling at. It was empty.

'Come on, Scamper,' said Peter, reaching for his collar to put his lead back on.

But Scamper wasn't finished. He barked and jumped right into the hole.

'OOOOOOWWWWW!' a muffled voice yelled.

The inspector shone his torch into the hole again. 'There *is* someone down there!'

The mud started to shift and Mr Brown pulled a big plastic sheet off himself. He had a red straw in his mouth.

'Stay *right* where you are,' said the police inspector.

The man groaned and spat the straw out.

'Using that to breathe, were you?' said the police inspector. 'Smarter than you look then, I suppose!'

Scamper barked and jumped out of the hole.

'Scamper!' said Peter, giving him a big hug. 'Good boy!'

CHAPTER TWENTY-FOUR

A BIG SURPRISE FOR THE SECRET SEVEN

THE NEXT day, everyone except for Pam and Barbara turned up for the Secret Seven meeting at exactly 4 p.m.

'Is there anything to eat?' asked Jack as soon as he walked into the shed. 'I'm still starving after all that action last night.'

Janet smiled and pointed to the feast that her mum had set up to congratulate them. There were ham sandwiches, sausage rolls, cheese and pineapple on sticks, mini chocolate tarts, a huge Victoria sponge cake and a bowl of fancy dog biscuits for Scamper.

Jack's eyes almost popped out of his head. 'Now that's a victory spread!' he said.

'Well, you'll have to wait until the meeting's over,' said Peter. 'We've got some news!'

Jack grabbed a biscuit and stuffed it into his mouth anyway and sat down.

Everyone stared at him with their mouths wide open.

'*What?*' he asked, munching away.

No one had the heart to tell him he was eating a dog biscuit.

'We got a call from the inspector this morning,' said Janet. 'Apparently Mr Brown helped dig the foundation for the restaurant extension a few months ago. The police think that's when he must've discovered some of the Roman coins and told Mrs Brown. Then together they came up with the plan to pretend to be the Lockhearts. The inspector said the Browns arrived at the hotel before the Lockhearts and then kidnapped them before anyone in the village had a chance to meet them.'

'What about all the money in the freezer?' said Colin. 'Do the police know where it came from?'

Peter nodded. 'The police said the Browns are wanted in Ireland for a big scam they did where they pretended to be travel agents and stole loads of money from old people who thought they were buying cruise tickets.'

'Did the police find the treasure hoard?' asked Colin. 'Were they Roman coins after all?'

Peter nodded. 'The inspector said they found the coins and jewellery in the basement and that there were another two boxes full of Roman jewellery hidden in the attic. They also found a load of Roman coins under the ice at the very bottom of the freezer, underneath their getaway stash of cash. The inspector says that it might be the largest treasure hoard ever found in the UK. He said it might be worth *millions*! Experts from the British Museum are on their way to collect everything. They're almost as excited about the Roman skulls as they are about the treasure, the police said.'

Jack's eyes went wide. 'Wow! Who would have thought *the mystery of the skull* would turn out to be a *million-pound crime*!'

'That reminds me,' said Janet, smiling at George. 'Why don't you go and take a look under that old blanket over there?'

George looked at where his old burnt bike was covered by a blanket. 'Why?' he asked.

'Just do it!' said Janet, grinning from ear to ear.

George got up and pulled the blanket off his old bike. But it wasn't his old bike. It was another bike.

'It's second-hand,' said Janet. 'It's all we could afford. Barbara and Pam didn't have to pay for the hotel room after all, so we used my birthday money and some of Peter's savings too. Dad took us to get it this morning.'

'Do you like it?' asked Peter.

'*I love it!*' cried George. 'You guys are the best! Thank you!'

George sat on his new bike in the shed for the rest of the meeting. He couldn't wait to try it out.

'What about the real Lockhearts?' asked Colin. 'Are they OK?'

Janet nodded. 'The police inspector said they were held in that hotel room for a week but that except for being a bit shaken up they were fine and had been reasonably well looked after. The inspector says they've finally had a chance to look around their new home and begin to unpack and get settled in.'

'The Lockhearts told me last night that the Browns promised them that if they stayed quiet they'd be safe,' said George. 'Then they took three of their little dogs and threatened to have them put down if they tried to escape. The only reason they didn't find the littlest one is because the girl hid her up her jumper. So they didn't know she had him until the end.'

'I wonder where the dogs are now?' asked Jack.

'There was no trace of them anywhere in the hotel,' Peter said, looking down at his shoes. 'They'd had those dogs for over ten years the inspector said. They were a big part of their family. We'll probably never know what happened to those poor little dogs.'

Just then they heard scratching at the door. Scamper raised his head from Janet's lap and barked loudly.

'It'll just be Barbara and Pam,' said Janet, giving Scamper another dog biscuit. He deserved it!

Jack stared at the dog biscuit bowl.

'Late as usual,' groaned Peter.

Peter hoped Pam and Barbara weren't doing the witch thing again. He wasn't in the mood. He was too upset about the missing dogs.

'What's the password?' asked Peter.

'Just open the door!' said Pam. 'Our hands are *full*!'

Peter sighed. 'I told you the other day. We posted

you a letter with the *new* password in it. You need to use it if you want to come in!'

Barbara groaned loudly.

'THREE LITTLE DOGS!' yelled Pam.

Peter looked at Janet and shook his head. They obviously hadn't opened the letter yet. And they weren't even trying to take a good guess at what the password might be.

'NO!' shouted Peter, crossing his arms.

'Um . . . YES!' replied Barbara.

Just then there was a tiny bark from the other side of the door. And then another.

Peter stared at the others. It couldn't be, could it?

'Open the door!' said Colin, jumping up. 'Let them in!'

Peter opened the door. He couldn't believe it!

'Look who we found!' said Pam.

Everyone gasped. Pam and Barbara were holding three of the cutest little dogs ever. 'We found them at the pound,' said Pam excitedly. 'I couldn't sleep last night after George told me about the Lockhearts' dogs. Then I remembered what my uncle had said about hearing lots of dogs in the background when Mrs Brown called him and how it had sounded like she was in a pound. That's when I realised that she probably did call him from the pound. And that she went there to get rid of the Lockheart dogs!'

Pam was speaking at a hundred miles an hour.

'So, first thing this morning, I phoned my uncle and told him everything and he took me and Barbara to the pound and we found them! The man at the pound told us that a woman had dropped off three elderly chihuahua dogs a week ago and that no one had adopted them yet. So we explained what had happened to the Lockhearts and got the police to phone the pound and back up our story, and the police told them to let us take the dogs and deliver them back to their owners! We're on our way there now. We came to get you all first!'

Peter grinned from ear to ear. This was the best news ever!

'Let's go!' he said, ushering everyone out. 'We need to get these little guys back to the Lockhearts right away. They're going to be thrilled!'

Everyone rushed out of the door.

Everyone except Jack.

'WAIT!' he yelled after them. 'Did I just eat a *dog biscuit*?'

The others laughed.

'Come on,' said Janet. 'We'll have a feast when we get back. Let's *go*!'

Enid Blyton

is one of the most popular children's authors of all time. Her books have sold over 500 million copies and have been translated into other languages more often than any other children's author. She adored writing for children and wrote over 600 books and hundreds of short stories. *The Famous Five* books are her most popular. She is also the author of other favourites including *The Secret Seven*, *The Magic Faraway Tree*, *Malory Towers* and *Noddy*. Visit enidblyton.co.uk to discover more.

PAMELA BUTCHART

is the bestselling and award-winning author of the *Baby Aliens* young fiction series, for which she has won the Blue Peter Best Book Award 2015 for *The Spy Who Loved School Dinners* and the Children's Book Award 2016 for *My Head Teacher is a Vampire Rat*. She has also been shortlisted for the Laugh Out Loud Book Award (Lollies) and is one of the fastest growing children's fiction authors in the UK. Pamela has written a World Book Day book for 2018. Her second *Secret Seven* story will be published in 2019.